WITCH WITH A GRUDGE

WITCH WITH A GRUDGE

WITCH WARRIOR™ BOOK 2

TR CAMERON   MARTHA CARR   MICHAEL ANDERLE

LMBPN

DISRUPTIVE IMAGINATION

LMBPN Publishing
PMB 196, 2540 South Maryland Pkwy
Las Vegas, NV 89109

Version 1.00, June 2022
ebook ISBN: 979-8-88541-196-7
Print ISBN: 979-8-88541-725-9

DEDICATION

Dedication: For those who seek wonder around every corner and in each turning page. Thank you choosing to share the adventure with me. And, as always, for Dylan and Laurel, my reasons for existing.

— TR Cameron

THE WITCH WITH A GRUDGE TEAM

Thanks to our JIT Readers:

Christopher Gilliard
Dave Hicks
Wendy L Bonell
Dorothy Lloyd
Diane L. Smith

If we've missed anyone, please let us know!

Editor
SkyFyre Editing Team

CHAPTER ONE

Deputy US Marshal Cait Keane imagined the annoyance spilling out of her must be filling the car she shared with Clement Austin, her partner for the day's adventure in poor decision making. After capturing Carl Winston, who had killed Judge Gideon Meyer, presumably at the instruction of one of the two criminal organizations in town, she'd spent ten hours across two days trying to get the man to say anything useful. He had given her exactly nothing.

The other marshals had tried, including Chief Levitt, but the assassin hadn't been interested in discussing any topic other than his lunch menu. All in all, it was deeply annoying and tasted like failure, even though it wasn't a surprise. She mused, "Television and movies really don't do a good job of representing how hard it is to get a criminal to talk."

Behind the wheel of their parked unmarked sedan, Clement snorted. He was dressed in an athletic suit, as usual, brown today, but he wore no tie, and his collar-length blond hair was mussed. The sides were still slicked back with precision, though. She was increasingly certain that her partner had two sides, one straight-laced and by the book, the other somewhere on the continuum between wilder and wildest. He said, "Yeah. It would help if we were able to turn off the cameras and beat on them for a while, though."

Cait chuckled and touched her neck, noticing now the absence of her dragon necklace, where it had been in previous days; its presence had sparked attention. "Yes," she replied dryly, "wanton physical violence solves so many problems."

He grinned. "Glad you're coming around to my viewpoint. But, you know, maybe some time in Solitary will loosen him up."

"Has that ever actually worked in your experience?"

"Not with a professional. And I think we can be certain he is one."

She finished a cup of coffee and wiped an errant drop off her hands onto her black jeans. She'd dressed down for the non-office day, opting for a casual blouse and comfortable hiking boots, her straight red hair pulled back into a comfortable ponytail. Her new chief didn't seem overly concerned with putting restrictions on his people. *Of course, it's not like I'm stupid enough to wear this to a court appearance or on a judge's protection detail, either.*

A dozen feet away, Winston and a second prisoner, both clad in bright orange jumpsuits, were loaded into the rear of an armored van by a quartet of police officers. The pair clambered up awkwardly, the shackles at wrists and ankles making large motions challenging. They watched while the prisoners' restraints were attached to the floor by a guard seated inside with them until the door closed and cut off sight of their charge. A police cruiser pulled out first, followed by the van, trailed by another cruiser. For now, they all ran without lights or sirens. *And hopefully, it'll stay that way. A calm, orderly prisoner transfer would be a gift right about now.*

Clement pushed the pedal down, and their car slid smoothly into line at the rear, its engine larger than the average for its make and model. She asked, "Why are we doing this again?"

He kept his eyes on the road. "Prison transport is a marshal thing. You should know that by now. I think it was on the tests."

She resisted flipping him off with difficulty. "Maybe the versions I took were too advanced to include such mundane details." He snorted, and she continued, "But seriously, I could've driven up to Devens, found a spot to portal to, and taken them both straight there. Would have saved a lot of time and effort."

He shrugged, following the convoy onto the highway. "The regulations aren't up to date on magicals, apparently."

"The regulations are dumb."

His dark laugh conveyed his agreement that the rules which bound the marshals weren't always the most sensible things. "No argument. But again, it is what it is. Besides, maybe the ride will inspire him to talk. One last trip out into the countryside before he goes into the darkness of the hole."

She asked, "Is it really called the hole?"

"On television it is. That's good enough for me."

They passed out of Boston city limits without a problem and exited the highway onto a four-lane back road that cut the diagonal to the federal prison. She sighed, thinking again of her unsuccessful interrogation. "He covered his tracks annoyingly well. No one found anything to connect him to Rosetta, not even Sabrina."

Clement nodded. "Or the Dragons, although I agree with you. Those glyphs and his hanging out in Chinatown were almost certainly a ruse."

"Rosetta's a right bastard."

"True that."

Cait was about to reply when a concerned voice sounded in her head. "Five cars that look alike coming up behind you." Aza, her magical size-shifting dragon partner, was keeping pace in the air above the convoy. She'd spent the weekend explaining to him about drones, emphasizing the need to stay above them to avoid being spotted. They'd also worked out rules of engagement. A moment later, the clear plastic earpiece nestled in her right ear carried Sabrina's words. "My camera is showing suspicious vehicles to the rear."

Clement flicked his gaze first to the rearview mirror, then to the side, and said, "I see them. They just seem to be keeping pace. What the hell is that about?"

Sabrina replied, "The drone I'm using belongs to the police. It doesn't have advanced sensor functionality. I can't tell you any more than that."

The answer to Clement's question came roughly a full minute later. While their attention had been focused on the threat from the rear, the real danger manifested from ahead. Without any warning, three cars, all different makes and models, veered across the earthen boundary that separated the lanes of traffic and slammed into the two police cruisers and the van almost simultaneously, knocking them all off the road into a grassy field.

Clement stomped on the brakes and wrenched the wheel, putting the car into a skid. The moment it stopped, Cait was out of her door and moving toward the crashed vehicles with her pistol in hand. She'd expected the distraction cars would join in, but they continued, not stopping. She warned, "Be on the lookout for reinforcements." The others acknowledged her comment.

Two more cars pulled across the road and stopped, disgorging people with weapons. Gunfire drove her back behind the car door, and Clement barked a curse as bullets slammed into the sedan just over his head.

She said, "Cover me. I'll shield and go for the van."

"On it." He raised his pistol and pulled the trigger repeatedly as she left the car's safety behind, wrapping herself in two layers of force shields, one following the lines of her body, the other in an oval around it. The sound of powerful engines from the right caught her attention as she slid down the embankment from the road, and she spotted four inbound vehicles coming across an empty field.

She categorized them automatically. *Military derivatives, huge tires, extra heavy frames, ramming bumpers. Probably bulletproof.* They created a staggered horizontal line as they barreled toward her. A moment later, only three remained as Aza swooped down and breathed fire across one of them, his German-Shepherd-sized form capable of dispatching a sufficient gout of flame to immolate the vehicle and cause its battery to explode. Her eyes followed him briefly as he circled back for a second pass, the sunlight glinting on his rainbow-hued scales.

Then more cars screeched to a halt on the highway, and gunfire from them sent her diving to the side, tumbling down another small embankment into cover. Her instinct was always to avoid incoming bullets, as one never knew if they might be anti-magic. She called, "You okay?"

Clement replied, "Yeah. Morin, what's the situation?"

"They're all over the place." Then their infomancer cursed. "They just blasted the drone out of the sky. I already have another, one of mine, en route, but it won't be there for ten minutes at best."

Cait asked, "Austin, I haven't seen any movement out of the police cars, have you?"

"No. The initial impact seems to have taken them off the board." Cait recognized the cold edge in his voice as that of a professional in the zone, someone willing away the intense emotions of the moment so they could do their job. She responded in a similar tone, "I doubt they're using anti-magic bullets. I'm going to charge over, try to get Winston out of the van."

"Dumb idea."

"It's the only one I've got. You have anything better?"

"No. Hang on a sec." She could see just enough over the edge of her hiding spot to watch him open the trunk and extract an automatic rifle from it. "I'll do my best to cover you."

She nodded. "Going in three."

Off to her side, another vehicle detonated as Aza swooped past it. "Two dead machines," he crooned happily in her mind. Damn, it would be nice to be able to talk to him telepathically, like he does with me. A nice blast of fire would be a great way to dissuade them from trying to shoot me. She pushed all thoughts except running out of her head and raced for the van, which was lying on its side with several figures in black clothes and masks working at the rear door.

Shouts went up as she started her advance, and gunfire came at her. She cringed at their arrival, but they ricocheted from her shields, fortunately not anti-magic. *Seems other people don't associate magicals and marshals, either. Guess I should quit whining.* The bullets' impacts were minor annoyances individually, but collectively, they pushed her off her straight line toward the van. She muttered, "To hell with this," and blasted force magic into the ground, sending herself flying into the air, confident the shooters below would find her more difficult to hit while airborne.

At the top of her arc, a drone flew out of nowhere and slammed into her chest, knocking her tumbling downward. She managed to right herself and discharge a blast of force before her impact with the grass and dirt, dissipating most of her velocity, but she still struck hard enough that her ribs creaked. It took her several moments to recover her senses, then their car screeched to a halt on the road.

Austin said, "They just drove off with Winston. Let's go get him back."

CHAPTER TWO

Cait cast spells to amplify her senses, having a moment to focus on something other than imminent danger for the first time since the enemy vehicles had crossed the median. Present just on the edge of her awareness, Aza flew above the car as it hurtled after their presumably escaping prisoner. The cars wove through civilian traffic, never losing speed, and Clement did the same, calmly piloting the sedan through what amounted to a deadly obstacle course. He said conversationally, "So, I couldn't help but notice a bunch of trucks blowing up back there for no apparent reason."

Here we go. "Totally. Weird, right?"

His cough communicated his lack of respect for her non-denial denial. "Magic?"

"Sort of, but not mine. An ally."

She'd turned to look at him while they spoke and saw him nod. "Flying ally."

She nodded. "Yep."

"Who appears to be able to use fire."

Inwardly, she chuckled. "Yes. Quite." *A damn pyromaniac, more like.*

His eyes cut over to her. "Keane, do you have a dragon?"

Cait laughed. "Sort of."

He twitched the wheel, and the Charger moved in a serpentine through a trio of slower vehicles. "We're definitely going to resume this conversation later."

She grinned. "That'll be fun." Her attention returned to the road ahead as the car surged forward. They were only a half-dozen car lengths behind the convoy, which was down to six cars, judging by the number of vehicles traveling in close alignment. A flash of rainbow scales again preceded a sheet of fire that covered the rearmost. It spun and tumbled off to the side.

Clement jerked the wheel to avoid following it. His expression was calmer than she would've expected as he asked, "It's not going to miss and hit us, is it?"

She shook her head. *Hopefully not.* "No. The rules are that he can only attack vehicles without people in them."

"Seems restrictive."

Cait chuckled low. "He's a touch aggressive. We're erring on the side of caution for the moment."

Clement gestured ahead with his chin. "Five left, and four are arranged around the fifth. That's probably where our guy is."

She replied, "Pull up closer. I'll jump over, get inside, and portal us away."

"The thing's an SUV, not like a bus or anything. You can manage that in a relatively small vehicle moving at high speed?"

"I think so."

He scowled. "You *think*?"

Cait shrugged. "Yeah. If you have a better idea, I'm open to other options."

With a sigh, he expelled the word, "No."

"Guess we need to take out the two in the back, then."

He hit the controls to set the car into autonomous mode, instructing it to maintain a consistent separation from the centermost vehicle. "Can you tell your friend up there to attack the rear cars?"

She shook her head. "They have people in them. Plus, I can't communicate with him except by talking, and we haven't figured out how to make a radio stay on his scales. So that's a double no."

"Seems inconvenient." He pressed the buttons to lower the windows.

Cait drew her pistol and checked automatically to be sure it was ready. "It really is." As one, they leaned out their windows and fired a barrage of bullets at the trailing vehicles. The rounds smacked into the cars' skins, and answering fire came from their targets, forcing them back inside the vehicle. The bulletproof glass in the windshield spiderwebbed as bullets struck it. She asked, "Want me to hit it with a fireball?"

Clement growled, "No. I've got this."

The car accelerated, and she realized what he was planning. "Are you sure about this?"

He laughed, and she heard a touch of that wild edge in it. "I am the office's unparalleled billiards champion for a reason, Keane."

A witty reply failed to occur to her, so she just braced herself on strong surfaces with her hands and feet as he raced forward and performed a PIT on the right side of the leftmost of the two trailing cars. The sedan's right side slammed into the back left of their target, knocking it sideways to bash into the other one. Clement jerked the wheel hard to the right as the one he'd struck spun out in front of him, then back to the left to avoid the other vehicle as it slewed from side to side, trying to stay on the road. As he pulled into line behind the car carrying their prisoner, the driver of the back right vehicle lost the battle, and it tumbled to the side of the road, flipping over several times before finally coming to a stop on its hood.

Cait pulled herself out of the window, sitting on the frame, and reinforced her shields in time to keep herself from becoming perforated as someone in the target vehicle leaned out the window and unloaded a rifle at her. *This is so stupid, Cait. Why do you have to be a showoff?* She ducked her head and said, "Get as close as you can, keep it steady, and for God's sake, don't hit them."

Clement laughed. "I'll do my best. Also, this seems like an appropriate time to mention that you're a crazy person. Good luck, wacko."

She climbed onto the roof without replying. *You're not wrong.* Despite a great deal of practice at magic-assisted leaping, Cait still wasn't fantastic at it. She could spend an hour calculating the trajectories and still not get it right, so she made the choice she always did in situations like that: to act. She blasted magic against the roof of the car, sending her flying forward toward her quarry, trusting instinct to get her where she needed to go.

Her initial burst was a little too powerful. She whipped out bands of force to grab onto the back end of the car and brought herself down safely on the roof, facing backward. Bullets shot up through the metal at her feet, but she'd shielded herself completely, including a layer under her boots. Nothing penetrated, but all the jolts were painful. *Okay, now that I'm here, how the hell do I get in?* Aza dipped down to fly nearby, and she pointed and screamed at maximum volume, "Rear window, rip it off."

For a moment, he didn't seem to have heard her, but then his wings moved, and his body aligned itself in a long straight arrow, surging toward the car. He flapped his wings at the last second to arrest his flight and slammed his claws into the rear window, digging into the bullet-proof glass that wasn't an effective defense against a dragon's talons. He ripped it away and flew backward, dropping it safely off to the side.

Cait called upon her long-neglected gymnastics training, one of many skills that made up Delsanra's combat instruction, and did a handstand, gripping the edge where the back window met the roof. She twisted as she continued the move, tucking her body and leading with her boots as she half-tumbled, half-swung herself into the back seat. Her feet hit someone on the way in, smashing them forward to hit the back of the driver's seat hard enough to snap their safety restraint out of its holder.

She used a blast of force to knock the left-hand door off the vehicle, then yanked the man to the left and used more of the same magic to hurl him through the opening with sufficient velocity that he made it to the grassy strip in the middle before hitting the ground. As gunfire came from her right, she leaned back, matching the position of the man beside her, Carl Winston, the prisoner they were allegedly transporting.

She twisted and reached across with her left hand, grabbing the back of his head and pushing it forward, then punched through the space it created with her right, catching the other backseat guard in the side of the head. The impact dazed him, and she repeated it with two more punches, delivering all the power she could from her awkward position.

Cait slammed a wall of force in between the backseat and the front to intercept a spray of bullets from a machine pistol. To the shocked man beside her, she said, "Well, that was a little indiscriminate. I think they would've been fine with killing you." He didn't reply and in fact seemed not to be present, his head lolling as his eyes moved frantically from side to side. "Okay, this will hopefully work. If not, apologies in advance."

She twisted and cast a portal between their backs and the car seat, focusing hard to keep it moving at the same pace as the vehicle, and they fell through to land in her safe closet in Georgia. Then she wrestled him to his feet, opened another portal, and stepped through to outside Tufts Medical Center's emergency room. *Well, he's transported. Just not to where he was supposed to go.*

CHAPTER THREE

The rest of the day of the failed transport had been spent debriefing. Now, after a solid night's sleep with a snoring dragon at her side, Cait was back at Tufts. The main entrance held a security checkpoint, and she flashed her badge as she walked through, her weapon setting off the metal detectors. Beside her, Garrett Bradley did the same. He wore a dark suit but had opted against a tie. As always, his head was perfectly hairless except for his eyebrows. His relaxed gait made her conscious of her own restless energy.

The guards, who had jolted at the alarm, quickly silenced it and nodded with what she thought was appropriate respect for fellow protectors of the peace. Aza, around her neck in his disguised form, said in her mind, "You'd think they'd have those on the outside of the building rather than inviting the threat in before worrying about it."

She chuckled. "You're not wrong."

Garrett asked, "What?"

Cait shook her head. "Never mind. Talking to myself." She didn't see a reason to share Aza's constant presence with her colleagues, even though the fact that she had a dragon as an ally was now the talk of the office. That morning, Sabrina had asked for an introduction, and Cait had promised to put something together. *My hotel room is a little small for a party. I really need to find an apartment. I wonder if pet-friendly covers dragons?* She pressed the button to summon the elevator and said, "Have your contacts given you anything at all on the Roses?"

He shrugged and rubbed a hand over his bald scalp in what looked like frustration. "Oh, I've got all sorts of information about Rosetta and his gang. Just not a single detail that connects to our friend upstairs. If I didn't know better, I'd say my sources were talking around the subject on purpose. But the people I deal with aren't bright enough for that."

The doors opened, they walked in, and she selected the twelfth floor. "Well, I'd love to say Clement and I had more luck, but that's not true. I couldn't even press Wilson when I was in the car with him since he was all loopy." She scowled. "Or, for all I know, pretending to be loopy. I kind of loathe that guy."

The doors opened, and as they exited, they were stopped by another pair of guards, this time police on loan to the marshals. The two forces had a strong working relationship in Boston, to Cait's admittedly inexperienced eye. She'd mentioned that to Garrett on the way over, and he'd only laughed and replied, "Sometimes." Now she brought it up again as they walked down the hallway.

He nodded. "We've vetted several folks to find a few we

can trust. Policing is pretty much a lifestyle choice rather than just a day job, and if the government will pay the overtime, we can always get volunteers to help out."

"We didn't get along so well with the PD in my last place."

He gestured at the door on their left. "It happens. It's taken a lot of work to put together a decent connection here, believe me." Garrett opened the door, and she preceded him through. The room was standard for a hospital but private, with a wide mechanized bed off to the left, a small bathroom to the right, and a large TV mounted on the wall showing an action movie. Instruments and readouts proliferated, providing a constant flow of information about the room's primary occupant, glowing in the otherwise dimly lit environment.

At their entrance, a man in an expensive suit stood up from his seat in the corner. His scowl was all the confirmation she needed to know he was Winston's lawyer since he'd already registered objections to their visit in advance. He gave the spiel about his client's rights, and she nodded with a condescending smile. *I don't dislike all lawyers, but ones that represent scumbag killers aren't any better than the dirt on my shoes.* As if he'd heard her thought, Aza said, sounding excited, "I don't like that guy. Can I burn him?"

She laughed, touched her necklace, and whispered, "No," as she turned to face the figure on the bed. "Hello, Mr. Winston. You're looking a little better today than yesterday." He had a tight-fitting black cap covering his head, probably to help with headaches, and his eyes still seemed to be having trouble focusing.

He replied with an irritating smile, "Yes. I suppose I should thank you for rescuing me."

She rolled her eyes. "Really. You're going with the story that you were captured by strangers instead of being rescued by allies?"

Winston gave a slight shrug and answered in a monotone. "I've never seen those people before in my life." She'd cast the spell to boost her senses before they entered the hospital, and she could hear his heartbeat when she concentrated enough. It was steady, matching the readout that tracked it over his head, suggesting he wasn't lying. *Or that he's really good at it.*

"Quite a coincidence, then. Do you think it was your former employer, Leonard Rosetta, behind it? I mean, you failed him, so it's not out of the realm of possibility he might want to punish you for that."

His heart sped up as he replied, "I have nothing to do with the Roses, so I don't know what you're going on about."

She drawled, "Uh-huh. Right."

The lawyer interjected, "My client is being voluntarily forthcoming, Deputy Marshal. Perhaps you could maintain some level of professionalism?"

Garrett answered, "Oh, she is. For instance, you still have all your teeth. How about you sit down and shut up, Sparky." He and Cait had quickly discovered how best to play off one another, and they put that knowledge to good use when dealing with lawbreaking chuckleheads. *And those that defend them.*

The lawyer bristled but complied. Her partner turned toward the figure reclining on the bed and asked, "I don't suppose you want to tell us anything else, do you? Might go over well at your sentencing and all that."

Winston grinned and put his palms behind his head, relaxed. "Nah, I think I'm good. Thanks for dropping by, though. I really appreciate the emotional support."

Garrett shrugged. "We tried. Best of luck in prison. You'll find lots of Roses in there, too, probably with home-made thorns to use on you."

Cait said, "I just want to check out the room for security purposes." She opened the door into the bathroom, walked inside, and took careful note of her location, imprinting it into her memory. Then she came out, closed the door, and made a show of checking all the equipment. She smiled down at the patient on the bed. "Wouldn't want you expiring before you got to prison or anything."

He shut his eyes. "That's swell of you. Thanks tons."

She laughed. "Get well soon. The sooner you're mobile, the sooner we can make you someone else's problem."

Twelve hours later, Cait pulled a stocking cap over her face, the cowl of a hoodie up over her hair, and cast a spell to disguise herself. "To senses all, provide a wall; unrecognizable me, let it be." That invocation was one she'd created when she was younger, and it still was the best way to gather her intent for that spell. Still, she was glad that only her partner was there to hear her say it.

Aza watched her from the hotel bed. "You could take me with you."

She shook her head. "Sorry, Fire Face. If anything bad

happens, I'll just portal away. There won't be any fighting. Nothing you can do to help me."

"I could burn his feet. Slowly."

She laughed. "Okay, that *is* something you could do for me, but now that people know I have a dragon as a partner, we probably need to be a bit more circumspect than that."

He sighed and rolled over onto his side, stretching his legs out and flexing his claws. "So many of your problems would be solved if you just addressed them directly." He grinned up at her. "I could also bite him."

She walked over and ran a hand down his scales, something she'd learned he enjoyed as much as any cat might like having its fur stroked. "In the business, we call that 'leaving a clue behind.' It's not considered a good plan for those who wish to stay out of jail." He opened one eye, which was enough to convey his impression of her concern. She laughed and patted him once more. "Back soon."

Moving to a corner, she created a portal connecting to the bathroom in Winston's hospital room. She exited quietly since he was asleep. Another low incantation prevented sound from leaving the chamber, and she used a wedge of force magic to hold the door closed. Finally, she whispered the spell to enhance her senses again and took a moment to compose her mind, sectioning off parts of it to keep each separate spell running.

The magics she'd cast were generally undemanding, which was the only reason she could maintain that many at once, and even then, it had only come through hard training with Sashura. When everything was ready, she walked forward and slapped Winston with a gloved hand.

His eyes bolted open, and his heart rate shot up in alarm at the sight of her. His gaze traveled the room frantically. Then he scowled and said, "What is it, Keane?"

Damn. I figured fear would keep him confused. Although to be fair, if it was a real enemy, he probably wouldn't have woken up, and I'm the only magical marshal he knows. She replied, "Not sure who you think I am, Winston, but you can consider me your own personal demon. I want to know everything about your trip to Boston, including why you tried to frame the Dragons."

He laughed. "Or what?" He shook his head. "Seriously, Marshal, you're not all that clever. I knew what you were doing when you checked out the bathroom earlier. I've worked with and against magicals for a very long time, so cut the nonsense."

She wasn't stupid enough to comply, unsure whether he might be recording their interactions. Instead, she said, "Talk, or tonight you die."

He shrugged. "You don't seem like the type, but if that's how I've got to go, fine."

Damn, he's infuriating. She continued to ask him questions for several minutes more, sprinkling in threats, but he steadfastly refused to be alarmed. After his initial reaction, his heartbeat didn't even increase. Finally, with a growl, she returned to the bathroom and portaled back, flopping on the bed next to Aza. The dragon asked, "How did it go?"

She sighed. "I don't want to talk about it."

He snorted and snuggled his spine up to her. "Should have let me bite him."

The next morning, after calling the doctors to ensure he'd be discharged that day, Cait drove to the prison and arranged a landing location, a small, secure room where the anti-magic emitter that covered the zone could be deactivated without creating a significant security threat. A quick portal took her back to the hospital, where she entered through the front doors and used the elevators again so no one could connect her to the previous night's visit. Her prisoner was jump-suited and handcuffed, with Garret watching over him.

After contacting the prison to deactivate the emitter, she took the prisoner's arm, opened a portal, and dragged Winston through it to the prison. His lawyer had been yelling at her as they stepped through because she refused to bring him along. Winston laughed as the rift closed. "He's going to be ticked."

Cait shrugged. "We do prisoner transport, not scumbag lawyer transport." She hauled him to the intake area and pushed him into the hands of one of the prison guards. A short conversation confirmed he was headed for Solitary for an indeterminate but significant amount of time. She turned to him and smiled. "Last chance, Winston. We could get you into WitSec."

He shook his head, seeming unconcerned that he was about to be imprisoned. "Plastic surgery and hiding out forever in some gross small-town you guys stash me in? No thanks. I'm too pretty for that, and it would be deadly boring."

"Somehow, I figured you'd say that."

He grinned. "Looking forward to the next time we meet, Deputy Keane."

She replied, "'Deputy Marshal.' It's not the old West."

"Might as well be for people like us. Have gun, will travel. That old line."

"Unfortunately, your traveling days are done."

His smile widened. "Guess we'll see." He mimed tipping a cowboy hat to her. "Until then, Deputy."

CHAPTER FOUR

After a singularly unfulfilling week, Cait was more than ready for a long weekend. *Thank goodness I lined up these vacation days before I transferred and Chief Levitt honored them.* She slept a little, then spent time organizing her things and neatening her room. Aza watched her from the bed, not lifting a hand, or wing, or claw, or whatever, to help.

Cait said, "You must be the laziest dragon on Earth. Or Oriceran."

He stretched with a sound between a growl and a groan and rolled onto his back. He replied, *I'm conserving my energy for when I need it. Something you might take a lesson from, given all your constant running around doing things.*

Cait laughed. "Yeah, I don't suppose I can argue against that. Now, get your butt off the bed, and let's go see the family."

Her portal delivered them to the stone circle landing pad outside the house and her sisters ran out the door. Cait responded with a grin and spread her arms wide, but

Brianna and Aisling dashed to Aza, wrapping him in hugs and patting his scales. She scowled. "Oh, sure. Now that there's a dragon, I don't matter. Real nice, alleged family."

Brianna rose to her feet, brushed off her knees, and embraced her. She whispered, "Don't knock yourself down, sister. You *never* mattered."

Cait replied by punching the other woman in the stomach. Brianna disengaged, laughing. "Based on that shot, you're clearly weak with hunger. Come on in. We've been holding lunch for you."

They went inside, where her mother properly hugged her before heading for the dining room. Moira patted the chair beside her, and Aza jumped up into it. Cait rolled her eyes as she sat down across from him. Brianna pulled the top off a serving dish to reveal charred cubes of meat and flicked several pieces onto the plate in front of the dragon.

He grabbed one, snapped his head back to throw it into the air, and gulped it down on its descent. That earned a round of laughter, so he did it again and again, soaking in the adulation. Once his food was gone and the show was over, they settled in to eat. He climbed down off his chair, circling under the table, where he curled up with a sigh. She sensed his emotions rather than heard words, which fully conveyed his contentment. *Oh, to be a well-fed dragon.*

Cait asked, "How has it been, being in charge of the coven?" The other three women groaned simultaneously, making her laugh. "So, pretty much as expected, then."

Aisling nodded. "The politics are out in full force in a way I've certainly never seen before."

Moira shook her head. "Those undercurrents have always been present. They're just visible on the surface now." Her mother shifted her gaze to Cait. "The Mohans are refusing to engage with us, despite several efforts to try to bring them back into the fold."

Brianna interrupted, "Sore losers is what they are. Each of us has tried and wound up being ignored, at best. One of the daughters had a few choice words for me, too. Maybe you can take a shot at them."

Cait finished a bite of salad, swallowed, and replied, "I think they like me less than they like you all. After all, I'm the traitor who abandoned the coven."

Moira scowled. "No one thinks that."

She laughed. "Sure, they do. And I'm positive some of them say it out loud. It's typical political nonsense like you said." She shrugged. "Some folks you simply can't convince. What about the rest of the coven?"

Brianna replied, "Mom and I have been making the rounds. Most people seem comfortable with the change, although moments such as this always bring some uncertainty, right?"

Cait nodded. "Definitely."

Aisling said, "Now tell us what you've been up to." Cait shared the story of her week, including her frustrations over not being able to get answers from Winston, and felt better for having done so. As much as she complained about her family, the truth was that trips to see them were rejuvenating beyond her visits to Croagh Patrick for meditation.

Brianna said, "There is one notable thing, though. When I was in Westport yesterday picking up supplies, the place had a really strange vibe. The visitors were all acting normally, so I don't think it was any concern outside the town. But the folks who live there, especially the ones who run the shops, seemed on edge to me. Like they were all worried about something none of them was willing to talk about."

Cait's lips turned down in a slight frown. The coven's proximity to Westport was a benefit in terms of securing supplies and such, but also a detriment since problems there could wash over onto them. "Any idea what it's about?"

Brianna shook her head. Her expression told Cait her sister was more worried than she was letting on. "None. But it's weird."

Cait took her napkin from her lap, patted her lips clean, and tossed it on the table. "All right. Show me."

Cait changed her footwear to something more appropriate for a hike, then she and Brianna set out for Westport. Aza, still tired from the meal, had shrunk to the size of a chipmunk and was riding on her shoulder, hidden under her hair. Interspersed with tiny snores were reflexive digs of his talons into her shirt as he unconsciously maintained his balance. Once they were beyond the coven's boundaries and several minutes into the forest, she said, "Okay, tell me how things *really* are."

Brianna laughed. "You think we'd lie to you?"

"I think Mom has an overprotective streak you're starting to emulate."

Her sister shook her head with a grin. "Nah. We've told you the truth about how the coven is reacting to its new leadership. Mom is a little stressed, as I'm sure you noticed, but also reveling in the chance to help the community in a more influential way."

Cait nodded. "I knew she'd be great at it."

"There was never a doubt."

She didn't notice anything out of the ordinary as they emerged from the forest into the periphery of Westport. But as they moved from the fringes into the town's main area, she caught a sense of what her sister was talking about. A wariness tainted the normally jovial atmosphere in town. When they stopped in to buy sweets from the chocolate shop, the proprietor, a friend of her family's for decades, treated them with a restrained neutrality that felt wrong. When they walked back onto the street, Cait asked, "Okay, I see it too. Do you think it's because of the new leadership?"

Brianna didn't reply, and Cait looked over to see her sister's gaze moving around. Her body was tense in a way that suggested she was looking for danger. "Bri? What's wrong?"

Her sister relaxed. "Nothing, I guess. Anyway, I don't think it's just because of the change. I was here the day after the vote, and people congratulated me and sent kind words for Mom, seeming quite positive about it. This is an odd reversal from that." They moved through several shops, gently probing the workers about what was going on in town but had nothing to show for their efforts after forty-five minutes.

Cait said, "Okay, I need to sit down for a bit."

Brianna laughed. "The city has made you soft."

"Bite me, Sasquatch."

Her sister laughed louder and opened the door of the Gallery, one of their favorite places in town. It was tiny for a business, with only four couches, a couple of tables, and a pair of comfortable leather chairs available for patrons. They ordered drinks and dropped onto a couch that faced the large front window.

Aza suddenly jumped from her shoulder onto one of the nearby bookshelves that covered the walls. A stone gargoyle was perched on the edge, and the miniature dragon crouched and imitated it, matching its glare. Cait laughed loudly, and Brianna accidentally huffed part of the iced tea she was drinking, resulting in a fit of coughing.

Her partner took that as positive reinforcement and flitted from shelf to shelf, imitating sports trophies, sculptures, and at one point, a portrait of the ancestor who had opened the business in the first place. Cait and Brianna were in hysterics by then, and the owner and a couple of other customers had joined in to watch, as a dragon wasn't something you saw every day, much less a miniature comedic one.

In a moment of transition from one bookshelf to the other, Aza landed in a flurry of movement on the edge of the couch, spread his wings, and hissed at the window. It was the most aggressive sound she'd ever heard the dragon make. Her eyes went to him in shock, then back to the window, following his gaze.

A flash of reddish hair was all she saw. She was on her feet, moving for the door before her brain caught up with her body. Aza flew out over her head as she broke into the street and headed after the red hair. After several minutes of running and scanning, she slowed to a stop at an intersection with no idea which way to go. From above, Aza flew down toward her, saying, "I'm not sure where he went."

She replied, "It was a man?"

Aza said, "Yes, but not a normal one."

"What do you mean?"

Brianna asked, "What's he saying?"

After Cait told her, Brianna sighed. "That's what I was afraid of."

Cait, exasperated, demanded, "What?"

"Shifters."

CHAPTER FIVE

Cait and Aza departed earlier than usual for the trek to Croagh Patrick. They arrived at its base with some light remaining, and she led the dragon up the path she remembered—the one that had taken her to find him. Her magically enhanced senses revealed none of the markers from before, and after several backtracks and retries, she acknowledged she wasn't going to be able to locate it. In truth, she didn't have a particular reason for searching for it other than curiosity and perhaps stubbornness. *So maybe quit wasting your time, doofus.*

She led the way back to the route that wound up to the summit. Aza trotted comfortably beside her, the solemn atmosphere of the historical mountain apparently inspiring him to silence, as it always did her. When they reached the top, she set about cleaning up the circles, restoring the stones that had fallen or been moved, and retrieving firewood.

While she did so, Aza paced inside each, sitting with his eyes closed at times, dashing quickly from one to the next at others, and walking almost in a meditative state within each. Finally, as she was about to set up the fire in the circle closest to the village, the one she traditionally used, she asked, "Aza, what are you doing?"

He replied, "Exploring. This circle," he fluttered his wings to indicate the ring he stood in, which was roughly in the center of the summit, "is the most connected."

"Connected? What do you mean?"

He gave her a slow blink, which was one of the signs she'd come to recognize as the equivalent of being patted on the head indulgently. "I feel Oriceran most strongly here."

"So, the rings' power comes from Oriceran. That makes sense. I didn't really consider it before."

He nodded, and there was humor in his voice when he replied, "Someday, you'll be as smart as a dragon. Maybe. If you work at it."

Cait threw one of the smaller sticks at him in a soft arc. He leapt out of the way and took to the air, flying lazy circles overhead as she stacked logs into a triangle in the middle of the ring he'd recommended. When it was ready, she called, "Let's go." He landed in the circle next to her and paced at her side as she walked the inner perimeter, whispering words of power.

When she knelt, made a final gesture, and said, "*Connigh*," the wards snapped up over them. They would protect her and Aza from anything that might threaten them. She smiled at her partner. "See you in a bit."

Her closing eyes shut out the world, and her senses turned inward. Time became meaningless as her mind traveled unfamiliar paths, exploring thoughts and experiences that hadn't reached her consciousness. Her meditation sessions on the mountain were a refresher for both body and mind and likely the only thing that kept her out of a constant state of stress-monkeyness.

Her reflection led her to a consideration of how she'd been using her magic, and she noted her increasing ability to reduce the length of spells, to allow one word to stand in for many. Eventually, she wouldn't have to encode her intention in words, Sashura had said, but would be able to trigger her magic with mental effort and a flick of her wand, like she did force magic, lightning, and fire.

As it did every time she thought of her magic, the question of whether or not she was limiting herself unnecessarily by not pursuing shadow magic crossed her mind. Again, as she did every time, she dismissed it. Sashura had intimated she would be willing to teach that skill if Cait wished to learn. But, so long as the idea made her uncomfortable, she would continue to choose not to. Her inner voice, which was usually muted during her meditations, asked, *Or are you just afraid of it and making justifications?*

Either way, the result is the same. I have no desire to do it now, and no need to.

Better keep training with the stuff you're good at, then.

Shut up. Her thoughts drifted deeper until finally, she entered a state of no mind and simply floated.

Nine nines, or eighty-one minutes, later, her eyes snapped open, the transition from meditation to alertness instantaneous. She noted two things. First, she felt even more rested and refreshed than usual. *Thanks, Aza. Good call on the circle.* Second, another being was on the mountaintop with them. The spectral fox sat just outside her wards, staring at her. Aza was asleep, either unaware of or unperturbed by their visitor. She whispered, "Rise and shine, Scale Snout."

He stretched and climbed to his feet with a groan. "You should really stop trying to make jokes. You're so not good at it."

She spoke the words to admit the fox to the circle, then closed it again, allowing him free travel. He sat primly, facing Aza, and gave him a nod that seemed respectful. The dragon returned it, then the creature turned to her, its red and black fur shining with magic. "It is heartening to see the two of you together as you should be."

Cait nodded. "Thank you for making that possible."

"It was my pleasure."

She sat cross-legged. "Has the danger you spoke of to the coven or to me changed now that we've partnered?"

His muzzle moved from side to side as he replied, "It has not."

Aza sent, amused, *Not very talkative, is he?*

The fox turned to face him and answered, "I communicate what I can."

Cait said, "You can hear him?"

"Of course."

"How?"

The fox smiled. "He is magical. I am magical." He offered no more as if that explained everything.

Turning back to the question that held the most importance for her, she asked, "Are the shifters part of the danger you mentioned?"

A solemn nod. "They are."

She sighed away the surge of anxiety that confirmation produced. "What can you tell me of them?"

He replied, "They are wolves. Once, their kind was common in this land. Now, they are not. These are the ancestors of the ones who once lived here."

Cait considered what it would be like to lose her village and found herself in sympathy with the shifters. "And they're not pleased about being pushed out or driven away, I'm guessing."

The fox nodded again. "You guess correctly. Whether they were, in fact, forced out is a question that no longer matters. They believe it is true."

Aza asked, "Why are they a threat? This land is large, and it seems to have sufficient forest for all. And if not, there is always Oriceran."

The fox replied, "This was home to them, and they feel a connection to it. They are instinctively territorial, as most predators are. Unfortunately, over time, they have adopted the worst elements of non-wolves and have now embraced the impulse to add more territory. To prey upon others, including those not normally subject to them. To rule."

Cait winced. Aza said, "You're saying they're evil."

The fox replied, "No. Good and evil don't apply to this situation. They have beliefs about their survival that they feel work well for them, and they are committed to them. Those beliefs function less well for others."

"So, either they've revealed themselves to the people of Westport, which I doubt since someone would've said something, or they're just a presence causing them concern."

The fox nodded. "That seems logical."

She asked, "Are the people of Westport in danger?"

He replied, "Yes."

"The coven?"

"Yes."

She forced down the lump of fear that had risen into her throat. "My family?"

The fox nodded, his expression as serious as she'd ever seen it. "As you are the leaders of the coven, and the coven serves as the magical protectors of Westport, most certainly."

CHAPTER SIX

The next day Cait felt energized, despite, or maybe because of, the fox's warning. She had planned to go with her sister to Westport, but when she was getting ready to leave, she had been sought out by one of the coven's children. After receiving her message, Cait announced, "Apparently, Delsanra wants a slice of my time today, and it starts now."

Brianna laughed. "No problem. I'll hit Westport myself."

"If you see shifters, you come back fast."

Her sister gave her a wry smile. "What, you think I'm going to get the coven involved in a war because I can't control my temper?"

Cait laughed and replied in a dry monotone, "I would never, ever, think such a thing." She shook her head. "No, but really, it's possible they'll try to manipulate the situation to start one. We need to make sure the opening they seek is impossible to find."

Brianna hefted the shillelagh she carried as a walking stick. "No worries. Self-defense only."

She replied, "And then only if they won't let you run."

Her sister blew out an exasperated breath. "Yeah, yeah. Whatever." She waved, grinned, and turned to stride at speed toward the forest.

Aza, who had been rolling around on his back in the grass waiting for them to get moving, said, "You don't really think she'll lose her temper."

Cait replied, "No. She's too smart for that. But it's amusing for us both to pretend she's not."

He rose to his feet and shivered, his scales rippling from head to tail, shifting from the dark green tones they'd picked up while he was sleeping to their normal metallic hues. "You people are weird."

She ignored the jibe. "Is the camouflage thing instinctive? Or automatic? Or what?"

Aza smiled at her. "All of that. Sometimes I have to think about it. Other times, it seems to happen when it needs to."

"And as long as it works, you're not worried." He nodded. "You don't worry about much, do you?"

"Nope. Most of the problems in my life can be dealt with by flying away or fighting. I welcome either option."

Cait laughed and patted him on the shoulder. "Well, speaking of fighting, I need to change into my training uniform. Then we'll go see what Delsanra has in mind for us today."

When they reached the backyard of her teacher's house, he was seated cross-legged on the grass, waiting for them. He gestured for her to do the same. She complied, and Aza sat primly beside her, back legs tucked, front legs straight.

He was the size of a Great Dane. "Delsanra, this is Aza. Aza, this is my teacher."

Delsanra smiled. "I've heard about you. You're even more impressive than the rumors suggest."

Aza accepted the praise, clearly pleased. "Thank you. I have seen Cait fight. Your training is very good."

Delsanra shrugged. "I do what I can, but it is up to the student to fail, succeed, or excel."

Cait acknowledged the implied criticism. "I would have been over later. My sister and I had planned to check out Westport first."

He replied, "So training is less important than what you were planning to do?"

She pointed a finger at him. "None of that. It's hardly so simple a choice."

He laughed and rose smoothly to his feet. "While we warm up, tell me what your life has been like since last we trained."

Cait matched his movements, the light uniform she wore allowing her complete freedom of movement. When she finished sharing the tale of chasing down the killer and fighting in the unpredictable jungle of Boston, he seemed satisfied with her response. He said, "So. The greatest gain would be to focus today on mobile combat techniques, as you are now treading unfamiliar ground."

She nodded, body and mind centered from their shared efforts. "Yes, that makes sense."

"Then, to the forest, we go." He opened a portal and made a polite gesture for her to precede him through it. He followed, as did Aza. It closed behind him, and he said, "The village is due west. Your challenge is to get there." He lifted the single shillelagh he'd brought into a guard position.

Cait stepped back and raised her own. "And Aza?"

Delsanra shrugged. "Your partner may observe but not intervene."

Aza observed, *Lame*.

She chuckled inwardly and replied, "Yes, teacher."

"Then begin." He twitched his weapon to instruct her to make the first move, and she advanced with a shout. Her shillelagh sliced down in a full-speed diagonal attack from upper right to lower left, targeted at his shoulder. She never worried about striking her instructor. He had explained early on that he maintained a tight shield and any blow that made it through his active defenses would cause only pain, not damage.

She'd replied that she didn't want to hurt him, and he'd laughed. "If I am foolish enough to let you strike me, the pain will serve as excellent instruction to avoid doing so again." True to his words, she'd never landed anything more than glancing blows. He shifted to the side, raising his weapon to deflect hers as she tried to modify her attack path but allowing her to pass in front of him.

That was the response she'd hoped for, not for a second imagining that her swing would catch him. Their battles always required planning several moves ahead while being prepared to abandon a line of attack without remorse if the situation called for it. She whipped her shillelagh around her back in a blind block, catching his weapon as it sped toward her spine, and ran.

Cait leapt over a fallen tree, ducked under branches that sought to whip her face, and spun to avoid obvious spots where a band of force magic thrown in front of her would trip her if cast low or knock her unconscious if cast high. She doubted her teacher would use magic since it wasn't an acknowledged part of the challenge. But in games like this, official rules didn't exist.

Occasionally, she heard Aza flapping his wings over-head, but the canopy blotted out more of the sky than it revealed. After thirty seconds, sounds to her right caught her attention, and she spotted her teacher pacing her, running easily through the trees. Then he reminded her that expecting things was folly as he threw a knee-high shimmering wall of force in front of her.

She vaulted it on pure instinct and slid under the next one he created at face height. She knew the spells weren't intended as a primary attack, only to cause her to evade and expend her energy, and somehow that was more frus-trating than if he'd actually been trying to hurt her.

When he threw a six-foot-high obstacle in her way, she used force magic to blast herself into the air, careening over the barrier with windmilling legs to grab a tree branch and pull herself up onto it cleanly. She smiled in satisfaction and looked for another one to jump to.

A crack of wood sounded as he slammed her perch with his magic, and she tumbled out of the tree. She managed to wrench her body into the proper attitude, used force magic to redirect her fall and absorb some of the impact, and hit the ground running. *Well, that's an improve-ment. I didn't land on my face—this time, anyway.*

She broke into a clearing, searching for the next vector to head toward the village. A portal appeared unexpectedly, and her teacher emerged from it. She feinted left and went right, and he shifted to block her, then slid in, slicing his stick at her legs. She jumped over the blow, snapping out a kick at him. He batted her leg aside with an easy block. She twisted to land at the appropriate angle and blasted a back kick at him.

That one connected, striking his shield and knocking him several steps backward. She spun and whipped the shillelagh upward in another diagonal strike, but he stopped it with an upraised foot. He stomped down and ripped the weapon from her grip, then simultaneously kicked it away and snapped his own stick around in a blow at her head.

She added an extra layer of force to her hand and grabbed his shillelagh. The shock of the impact traveled up her arm, but the shield was strong enough to keep her from damage. *And pain teaches. Next time, two extra layers.* He twisted his weapon out of her grip, which gave her time to use telekinesis to summon her own back to her hand.

They traded blows and strikes in a flurry, Cait panting as she concentrated on trying to break through his defenses. An opening appeared, and she realized it was deliberate even as she reflexively tried to take advantage of it. He fell into a backward somersault, gaining distance, and she heard the new threat a moment before it reached her.

Aza's talons scraped the back of her uniform as she dove to the side. She came up swinging, pulling the blow to avoid hurting him when it connected with one of his trailing feet. He did a barrel roll, his laughter filling her mind, and came around for another attack. She raised her shillelagh defensively, prepared to strike as he passed. He angled to evade it but opened his mouth and breathed on her as he flew by.

She shouted, "Maybe brush your teeth sometimes, honestly," but the message that she could have been roasted where she'd stood had been received. When she turned back to her teacher, he was gone. Cait dashed into the trees again, running for the clearing at the rear of Delsanra's house.

She reached it without additional trouble, aside from some needed evasions and leaps, when he again paced her to throw more magic in her way. She slowed to a stop, breathing hard, and called, "I made it." It was with complete surprise that she then pitched forward, slammed to the ground by a heavy weight that struck her from behind, and landed on top of her. Brianna whispered in her ear, "You have to be ready for anything, sister." The other woman pushed Cait's head into the turf as she used it as a lever to climb off her.

Cait sat up, pulling a leaf out of her hair and wiping blades of grass from her lips. "That was dirty pool."

Delsanra, sauntering into view with Aza at his side, advised, "You must be prepared for the unexpected in the new city you've chosen. Now, get up and quit dawdling. It's time for you two and the dragon to train together."

CHAPTER SEVEN

After another hour spent training with her partner, which was pleasurable for everyone involved, Cait, Brianna, and Aza had trekked to a small lake at the bottom of Croagh Patrick and devoted some time to swimming and relaxing as much as was possible in the chilly water. It was there she discovered the dragon's wings made highly effective scoops as Aza sent cascades of liquid over Cait and her sister, who responded with blasts of force to dowse him.

She was tired when they reached the house, even after her refreshing meditation of the night before. With a brief stop to hug her mother and pat her younger sister on the head, she went up to her room, changed into shorts and a tank top, and settled in for a nap, the dragon at her side, again hogging most of the bed. His body heat and the solidity of his presence lulled her quickly to sleep.

Dinner was a comfortable affair, filled with good food and conversation. But an undercurrent of anxiety over things to come flickered at the edges of her awareness, radiating from her mother and her sisters. *I wonder if they know something they're not telling me or if this is just normal concern because of the responsibility we've accepted.* No one spoke of it, preferring to treat the meal as an oasis of comfort. But as she went upstairs to change, Aisling slipped up beside her and said, "Probably best to be ready for anything."

Cait replied, "Shouldn't you be at school?"

Her sister laughed. "Classes are over. Now it's just about finishing up my final project. I have a few weeks."

"Don't let family stuff mess this up for you."

"No worries. You're the one with the overdeveloped sense of responsibility, remember?"

Cait chuckled and headed upstairs. *Be ready for anything? Okay, then.* She selected jeans and her hiking boots, then slipped on a t-shirt with a leather jacket over it. The jacket was tougher than it looked. The material was treated until it moved and felt like something much less protective. She buttoned it up to her throat and pulled her hair into a fast warrior's bun, stabbing a pair of sharp hairpins through it to keep it secured. She considered her pistol but opted against it, leaving it in its lockbox. A gesture brought the walking stick leaning in the corner to her hand, and she headed downstairs, Aza a step behind.

The circle was mostly complete by the time they arrived and took the space reserved for the coven leadership. The former witch-in-charge, Sinead, led them through the lighting ceremony. Cait saw each rising ball of flame as a plea for good fortune sent into the universe.

When the ritual was finished, Sinead sat beside her daughter, and Moira took a step forward.

She smiled and paused for a beat to ensure that all attention turned to her. "Our community is gathered tonight to reaffirm our connection, to embrace the whole that we create, which is far stronger than the pieces that comprise it. At this time of renewal, as plants break the earth and stretch toward the sun and rain that spring brings us, we, too, must reach for what we need."

Cait kept her face impassive, but her mother's words and the way she delivered them made her want to smile. The love and care that Moira had always bestowed on her family now included the entire coven. She hoped they felt it as strongly as she did.

"The hardest part of that is admitting that we need anything. Some of us prefer to show a brave face or don't want to inconvenience others. This is unsustainable. We must be willing to share our strengths and our weaknesses, or we can never become all we are meant to be. So, I ask you—"

Her words were interrupted by a lone, ululating howl from the west. More joined it until the sounds were coming in waves, surrounding them completely. Brianna growled quietly, "Shifters." Cait nodded and gripped her shillelagh farther down the haft, turning it from balance support to a useful weapon.

The howls faded, and a figure stepped into the circle's illumination. Cait whispered the spell to enhance her senses and saw him clearly. His face was strong and angular, with a well-trimmed beard covering it. He looked to be in his forties, and both his facial hair and the long locks that cascaded down over his shoulders had strands of gray among the chestnut brown.

His clothes brought her fighting outfit to mind. Tight leather pants covered him below the waist, and a matching vest hung open over the bare skin of his torso. His feet were naked. Dark tattooed whorls decorated his arms from shoulder to wrist.

Aisling said, "I didn't hear him coming, and I was listening."

Magically, she meant. *Like I should have been.* "So, magically silenced or concealed. Which means more of them could be nearby."

From around her neck, where he was pretending to be a necklace again, Aza offered, "I don't sense any. I think he's the only one close."

She whispered, "That's reassuring. Keep an ear out."

"Always."

Moira stepped into the open center of the circle opposite him. The coven shifted position to create a lane connecting them, and both Sashura and Delsanra moved near it, about halfway between her mother and the newcomer. Brianna made a move to step forward, but Moira held up a hand to stop her. Her mother's eyes locked on the man's as she spoke. "Greetings. I am Moira Keane. How may we assist you?"

His voice was lower than she'd expected it to be, based on his looks. With a calm confidence, he answered, "By leaving."

Cait exchanged a look with Brianna, then circled around the fire to stand on the far side of her mother as her sister took the shorter path to the near side. Moira replied, "This is our home and has been for generations. We have no enmity toward anyone and seek to live in peace."

"We have enmity toward you. And you may continue to live in peace, so long as you do it somewhere else. This place belongs to us, as it did before you came." Cait noted that the man's hands were knotted into fists. *Not quite as emotionless as you pretend to be, are you?*

Brianna said, "By what right do you make such a demand and claim?"

He replied, "By the only one that matters. Might."

Cait spoke in her marshals' de-escalation voice, which had prevented violence in any number of standoffs. "Perhaps a middle ground can be found if we put our minds to the problem together?"

The grin the man offered her was so condescending that her left hand ached where it gripped her stick. "To stay means your death. So, by leaving, you live. If you consider that to be a middle ground, then yes, we have found it."

Aisling, who had moved up beside Brianna, replied, "You understand it's not the Middle Ages, right? In the modern world, you can't just simply come here, demand we leave, and expect that to happen."

"In our world, we can. That is enough. You've been warned. We will permit you some time to get your affairs in order before we move on to more," he paused and smiled, showing his teeth, "direct methods of persuasion." He turned his back to them and walked away to another chorus of wolf howls.

The remainder of the gathering was spent discussing the new threat to the coven. Then, as it broke up, fully a third of the group remained behind to talk directly to them. They each did their best to reassure the coven that, whatever came, they would handle it together.

When they finally made it back to the house, they quietly changed into comfortable clothes, brewed herbal tea, and pulled several tins of cookies out of the cupboards. They sat around the table and filled mugs and plates. Cait broke the silence. "Last night, when I was up on the mountain, I was visited by the same creature that led me to Aza. He said that the wolves did, in fact, inhabit the island before they were pushed out by people demolishing their forests. He also confirmed that they were the threat he had referred to before."

Moira nodded. "The existence of the shifters is a secret that Sinead held and shared with me after the coven selected us to lead them."

Brianna asked, "How shall we respond?" Cait was impressed that her first question wasn't to ask why their mother hadn't shared the information.

"Deliberately."

Her sister nodded. "We also need to increase our protection. And Westport's."

Her mother nodded. "Yes. Brianna, you make that happen. Aisling, you find technological ways to help."

A nod of confirmation accompanied her younger sister's "Yes."

Moira turned to her. "Cait, there's nothing for you to

do right now, but be ready since we may need your help at a moment's notice."

With a reluctance born of knowing how likely that would be to interfere with her actual job, Cait said the only thing she could. "Yes."

CHAPTER EIGHT

Yoshino Kyouka, the leader of the criminal organization known to English speakers as the Dragons, watched the storefronts go by from behind tinted windows in the rear seat of a limousine. She was willowy and could easily be overlooked so long as she remained quiet and focused her will on keeping her energy inside. Her body was covered by a slim-fitting black pinstripe business suit with a dark red blouse, and her long, straight black hair, which would normally be highly styled for a gathering with her people, was drawn back in a simple, executive ponytail.

She had just come from a meeting with the board of directors for a bank in which she held a minority interest but a level of command that was far greater. She knew the importance of first impressions. *It would not do for them to see me in finery appropriate to my true station, which they would denigrate as traditional and weak.*

Yoshino was anything but weak. She had risen to prominence in a criminal underworld ruled by men, despite the need to prove at every turn that she was thrice as capable in order to accomplish half as much. Her ascent was bloody, merciless, and pragmatic. Publicly, she followed the rules, only changing them where necessary to accommodate her gender. She adhered to the traditional expectations, which were necessarily violent, as any sign of disagreement or lack of loyalty must be instantly expunged, ideally by the leader's own hands.

Behind the scenes, though, she made deals with those who others would not stoop to engage, including members of every race and social class present in Boston. Her own ancestry, equal parts Chinese and Japanese, allowed her to bridge gaps her competitors could or would not. *It also causes them to underestimate me, again and again, which is to my advantage.*

She dismissed her reverie as the limousine pulled up to the curb in front of the Xin nightclub, her most well-known base of operations. It was here she met with her subordinates, here she allowed petitioners to request appointments to speak with her during the evening hours on certain days. The remainder of the time, she was mobile, moving from one of her places to the next. That made her a difficult target for those who might seek to remove her as part of their own rise to power.

The club was in a four-story building in Chinatown's entertainment sector. When she entered to bows from the workers at the door, the music and press of humanity hit her like a wave. She allowed it to wash through her and reveled in the sheer sense of life present in the place.

Rather than continue into the first-floor throngs or the more relaxed areas of the second level, she turned to a small elevator on the right-hand wall. It opened at her approach, and she and a single bodyguard stepped inside, that being all the lift would accommodate. No one save her and her closest defender, Saito Iwaki, used the elevator. The rest of her guards, and the underlings who had been summoned to meet with her, would have to use the stairs. She knew, thanks to hidden electronics that surveilled those of her inner circle, that they found the climb up to the third-floor demeaning. *Which is the point.*

The top level, effectively insulated from the sound of the club below as well as the level directly underneath, was her private refuge, the one she most favored. The elevator opened onto a back hallway with dark wood paneling, a tile floor, and an off-white ceiling with indirect light. An area for her private food preparation, which she never visited, trusting her staff for such tasks, lay to the left. A sliding screen to the right separated the bedroom from the corridor. She rarely slept in it, as her association with the club was too well-known.

The next door from the hallway opened onto a dressing chamber with more than enough space for her needs. The corridor ended at the main section of the apartment, a large living room filled with elegant furniture adorned in red, black, and touches of gold, as most of her reception spaces were.

She turned into the dressing room and closed the door behind her, knowing Saito would block any entry. She methodically removed the business suit and set it carefully on the table reserved for items to be dry cleaned. Dressing was a slow process, as she used the donning of each piece of her outfit as a moment to center her thoughts and wall away her concerns.

While the final product would appear traditional from the outside, it was less so underneath. She slipped on a pair of tight pants that included a layer of metallic weave that would hinder bladed weapons and unarmed strikes. A shirt of the same material that overlapped the top of the pants by six inches covered her from the base of her throat to the middle of her forearms.

The next additions were fashionable boots that reached to mid-calf and an inner robe to conceal the base layer. Within it lay cunningly concealed sheaths, and she slipped a pair of thin knives into them, last resort weapons she had never had occasion to use. When she had been forced to wound or kill with her own hands, she had used a sword, or on very rare occasions, a gun.

Over it all went a formal silk outer garment adorned with a purple version of the creature that gave her organization its name. She released her hair from its ponytail and wove it into a tight bun, leaving trailing pieces to balance its severity. A pair of ivory hairpins, themselves effective weapons in a moment of need, secured the arrangement. As she slid the second one into place, her mind was centered, and she was prepared for the meeting. She opened the door and stepped out beside her bodyguard, who had moved out of her path at the first sound of her emergence. She asked, "Do I look the part?"

Saito had seen her in all her disguises; he had been a constant presence since the beginning of her rise to power. He always looked the same, with his hairless face, dark, precisely trimmed businessman hair, and black suit, shirt, and tie. His only flair, if one could call it that, was the thick silver cuffs hidden at his wrists under his shirtsleeves. He inclined his head respectfully. "You are very beautiful, Madam."

Yoshino smiled. "And you are a flatterer."

He chuckled, showing straight white teeth. "It is effortless to compliment when one has such loveliness at hand."

She rested her fingers on his arm. "Shall we?"

They returned to the elevator and took it down one floor. It opened into an office, and as the door closed, all evidence of the lift's existence vanished behind the wood paneling that slid into place, matching the rest of the walls. She ran a practiced eye over the room, ensuring the tools she might need were present on her desk, that the bar cart at the side was stocked, and that the samovar with hot water for tea had a flame beneath it. All was correct, as she expected it to be, and as it invariably was.

Yoshino sat in the large chair behind the desk and pressed a button inside one of the drawers. Panels slid away to reveal monitors on the walls. She said, "Conference room," and the security staff, who were always listening when she was in this room, activated the cameras she'd requested. All her top-level underlings, other than her second in command, who was out on another task, were gathered as she had ordered, seated around the long conference table that was much larger than this meeting required. Notably, none of her guests had sat next to another, and none were at the right or left hand of the seat at the head of the arrangement. She chuckled. "They're nervous."

Saito replied, "Justifiably so, given recent events."

She gave a sharp nod. "Well, then, let's not keep them waiting."

At her entrance, the people around the table rose and inclined their upper bodies in respectful bows. Her eyes roamed the room, which was styled like any executive meeting space. An ornate credenza lay to one side, a video display awaited commands on the far wall, and the entire chamber was filled with metal, leather, and steel accents.

She squinted a little against the illumination and made a small gesture toward it. The lights dimmed slightly in an immediate response. She lowered herself to sit on the edge of her seat with her back straight and her hands folded on the table. The others also returned to their chairs.

Their struggles to keep their eyes from locking on her for any sign of danger amused Yoshino. She said, "I have an important question for each of you. You have all been informed of recent events. The assassin who eliminated Judge Gideon Meyer was found in one of our clubs and was chased through our streets. Thus, the first and most vital truth we must ascertain before we can make any plans is this: Were you involved?"

Each of her underlings in turn vowed they had not been. Their verbal confirmations were unnecessary since her guards had been investigating them more intensively than usual since the event. *Likely, they're aware we are doing so, as well.* But she was talented at identifying lies and was gratified to recognize none. "Very well. I believe you. Please tell me what you know about these occurrences."

A man to her right, wearing a business suit with an emerald tie and sporting an impressive Fu Manchu mustache that contrasted notably with his shaved head, replied, "A review of security footage shows the assassin visited the club for several nights in a row. It is my belief this was a deliberate attempt to ensure he was found there if he was to be discovered or traced to the location."

Another at her left, older and with a scar running down his cheek, growled, "Clearly an effort by our enemies to implicate us in something we did not do."

Yoshino asked, "Why do you believe Rosetta would do such a thing at this time?"

The only other woman in the room, tall and willowy, with collar-length black hair and makeup that caused her face to appear stark and angular, replied, "Perhaps the organization has secured new connections and is putting them into play. It is my understanding the assassin is part of the Syndicate."

That revelation rippled around the table, another indication that her people's loyalty was untainted. Yoshino inclined her head at the woman in acknowledgment of her contribution. "We will need to investigate, to be certain. What connections do we have with the syndicate?"

The eldest member of her organization's leadership, a heavyset man with a white dagger beard and thin mustache, replied, "I have had dealings with them in the past, before coming to the United States. It was decades ago, but it is possible some of the contact pathways still exist."

Yoshino gave him an approving nod. "Excellent. Reconnect with them and arrange for a representative to meet with me."

Reluctance flickered across his face, but his voice was

steady as he replied, "That may prove difficult. They are prideful and expect others to come to them."

She offered him a thin smile. "I trust you will find a way." Then, turning back to look at her gathered subordinates, she said, "While we may hope for revelations from this avenue of inquiry, a more direct route exists that we cannot ignore. The assassin himself."

Nods went around the table. Members of their organization could be found in all the nearby prisons, and in many others as well. She continued, "I need not know how it will be accomplished, but I expect that this man will be delivered to me within the week. You will work together to make it happen." She rose, and they did the same. "As always, failure shall result in significant consequences." Yoshino said the words with a smile. *Love me or fear me. All that matters is that you obey me.*

CHAPTER NINE

After the strangeness of the weekend, it was reassuring to be back in the office. Cait dumped her stuff on her desk and headed to the conference room for the weekly staff meeting. She looked forward to focusing on her other set of responsibilities for a while, confident the shifters wouldn't undertake any moves against the coven in the near future. *Of course, it's an old adage that when you make plans, the universe laughs.*

Chief Levitt sat beside Clement on one side of the oval table. The office head wore his suit like he'd rather be in sweats, and his white hair, as usual, was unwilling to stay where he'd styled it, sticking up here and there. Garrett dropped into his seat next to hers a moment after she sat down. Sabrina arrived last, rushing into the room with an apology. Simon only smiled at his people and asked, "So, how were your weekends?"

Garrett replied, "Baseball's starting up. The kids are practicing, allegedly getting themselves ready for actual competition. Naturally, that involves massive stress, tons of complaining, and lots of prisoner…I mean *child*, transport."

Clement laughed. "Well then, I have to say, I think I had a better weekend than you did. I went camping with a few friends. We were out seeking good hunting spots for when bow season starts."

Cait replied, "You're a bow hunter?"

He nodded with a grin. "Every weapon is a friend of mine. I love them all, though not equally." They laughed.

Sabrina, sounding almost embarrassed, said, "I took second place in a battle tournament online. I'm climbing up the rankings."

Garrett asked, "Is that an infomancer thing?"

The other woman shook her head. As always, she was in a black dress, but today her black hair was hanging down her back in a braid. "Nope. Just a video gamer thing. I may have an advantage since I have a really good connection and a high-end machine, but it's mostly about skill… along with a smattering of luck. I've got a decent amount of the first, not as much of the second."

Cait asked, "Can I watch sometime?"

Sabrina flashed a grin. "Of course. I'd love that."

Aza, in his normal position around her neck, whispered in her mind, *We should go hunting with Clement. You shoot it. I'll cook it.*

She patted the necklace, which was all she could do to respond to him. Simon said, "I spent my weekend at a technomagic seminar, learning about how the field interfaces with law enforcement. Pretty cool stuff, although I only understood about half of it. How about you, Keane?"

Cait shrugged. "Visiting family. The usual." *Understatement of the season.* "Any news on Winston?"

The chief shook his head. "None."

"Dammit."

"Yeah. That guy's got some serious resistance. Not surprising if he really is part of the syndicate." He sighed in frustration. "Before I forget, the fugitive list has been updated since we took one off. Congratulations from the director on that, by the way. Be sure to review it."

He tapped the tablet on the table in front of him and asked, "Any questions or concerns other than Winston?" The room remained silent. "Good. Continuing the theme of irritating news for Monday, we got an order from above to review building security from top to bottom."

Garrett and Clement groaned. Cait asked, "Why?"

Simon shrugged. "Like I said, 'Word from above.' That usually doesn't come with an explanation, though I'm sure there's a good reason behind it." His sarcastic tone suggested the opposite. "If I had to guess, it's because of Judge Meyer's murder. There might've been a new threat sent in, but one would think they'd tell us about that if it was the case."

Sabrina said, "I haven't heard anything, and info-mancers tend to gossip."

The chief continued, "Our area of responsibility is the courtrooms and the judges' chambers. So, since this is your first time in the building on this assignment, Keane, you're with Austin. Bradley and I will operate solo. Coordinate with Morin as you clear each area. Let's get to it."

They rose and headed to the equipment room. In addition to their lockers and personal items, the space also held heavy weapons behind security grates, additional body armor, and a pair of locked cabinets secured to the walls. Simon tapped a code into the keypad on one, and it popped open to reveal black wands that looked vaguely like police nightsticks, with a textured handle, a small rectangular display, and a cylindrical detector the length of her forearm.

She recognized the devices from Columbus. They detected explosives, metal, and transmissions. Settings allowed the operator to select all three modes at once or in any combination. She swung hers at her side, testing its balance and reconfirming it wouldn't make a particularly good weapon as she followed Clement to the nearest courtroom.

She'd been surprised at how mundane and undecorated they were, compared to the ones they'd had in her previous city. When she'd mentioned that to Garrett one day, he'd shrugged and said, "It's a new building. All very businesslike and boring. Not even a single decently scary interrogation cell in the place."

The jury box was off to the left, a raised platform with seven seats in a row on each of two levels. The prosecution and defense tables stood beyond the rows of chairs that accommodated spectators. A large display took up one far corner, opposite and slightly diagonal from the jury, and the judge's bench dominated the front of the space.

It, at least, had a bit of the pomp and circumstance she recognized from her previous gig. She walked across the room to it as Austin devoted his attention to the chairs nearest the hallway doors. She turned off metal detection since there was *always* metal and explored for the other two first. The judge's bench held nothing out of the ordinary.

She switched the device to metal-sensing mode, but after careful inspection, she found none where it shouldn't be. Over the next couple of hours, they cleared the rest of their third of the courtrooms, finishing before Garrett and the chief. After a trip to the first floor for lunch, where several small food stands were set up, they returned to the fourth. Austin asked, "Where do you want to start?"

"How about Judge Meyer's chamber?"

"That's been investigated a bunch of times by now, I imagine."

She nodded. "But not by us."

"Fair enough."

They entered the room to find a large desk, an armoire, and a table that would seat six inside walls mostly covered with bookshelves and framed pictures of the judge with presumably important people. The armoire stood out. He must have added it since the large carved wooden piece didn't fit the decor of the chamber or the building. Behind the desk were several windows that looked over the water, and Cait shook her head at the view. "It's beautiful here. I really need to get an apartment."

Clement laughed. "You're still in that hotel room?"

She scowled dramatically. "I've been busy. You may have heard about me catching a killer."

He waved a hand. "Old news. What have you done for us lately?"

Austin moved to the armoire, and she chose the desk. She pulled open every drawer and moved the wand around inside, failing to find anything unusual. Then she crawled underneath to get a good look at the bottom. Nothing drew her attention. They stalked around the rest of the room, eventually coming up empty-handed, just like they had in the courtroom attached to it.

Cait had a feeling, or an instinct, or maybe simply a reluctance to admit defeat. She selected the radio function on her cell phone and said, "Sabrina, can we kill the anti-magic emitter in here?"

The infomancer replied, "I don't have access. I'll have to work through building security. Stand by." The presence of anti-magic emitters throughout the building was a necessity, and she'd learned to endure it in the Columbus courthouse. She didn't like it, as it cut her off from many of her best talents and left her feeling a little empty. *Wonder how Aza handles it? I should ask. Maybe, being a magical being, they don't affect him.*

After several minutes, Sabrina pinged her. "Okay. They wanted to post extra guards outside in case something weird went down. Everything's ready."

"Awesome. Do it."

When the anti-magic field vanished, it was like being able to breathe fully. She paused, indulgently letting herself enjoy the sensation, then clapped her hands. "All right." She cast the spell to enhance her senses, then spoke the invocation to detect living magic. Nothing revealed itself to either spell.

She released the second spell and cast one to detect inanimate magic, which had a different signature than living magic did. She walked slowly around the perimeter of the room, focusing intently on the spell. An itch encroached on her awareness as she neared the armoire, and she moved closer to it with growing excitement. The scraping against her senses intensified, but she couldn't pin down the source. "There's something on this thing, or in it. I can't get any better sense of its location. It's really thready."

They emptied the freestanding closet and ran their hands over every interior surface. When that revealed nothing, they pulled up chairs and did the same to the sides and the top. She used telekinesis to move the armoire away from the wall, and they checked the back thoroughly, again to no avail. Finally, saying, "This pretty much has to be it," Cait used her magic to lift the heavy piece of furniture, pushing it up against the ceiling so they could examine the underside.

Clement looked at her doubtfully. "You're not planning to drop this thing on me, are you?"

She laughed. "Only if you keep insulting me. This isn't hard, but it's not exactly easy, either. Do your thing."

It took him only seconds to find it, and he moved out from beneath the armoire with a hissed, "Yes." She set the furniture back down, and he extended his palm to her. In it lay a small square that radiated magic.

When she waved her wand over it, the device buzzed for both transmissions and metal. "Technomagical. Not sure how that's useful with anti-magic emitters always on.. Do they ever turn them off?"

Sabrina, who had been listening in through the phone Cait had set on the desk, replied, "For maintenance and testing once a week. Never more than one at a time."

Clement nodded. "It's probably a burst transmitter,

then. The emitter turning off activates it, and it sends all its information out in one data stream."

Sabrina growled, "This offends me on a personal level."

Cait replied, "Me too."

Clement sighed. "Not as much as it's about to."

She replied, "Why?"

"Because now you and I have to clear all the rooms again."

CHAPTER TEN

Cait braced herself as Clement's Charger took a harsh curve. They were on the road where they'd prevented Winston from being kidnapped, headed back to the penitentiary at top speed. In her earpiece, Sabrina said, "The prison is in lockdown. No other information is available." The alert had gone out only five minutes before. She and Clement were already outside the city on a different task.

She growled, "I should've identified a secondary location to portal to. Dumb move."

Clement's eyes didn't leave the road. "Second-guessing does no good. Always focus forward."

"You're driving. You focus forward. I'm going to sit over here and be irritated for a while."

He laughed, but aside from Sabrina's periodic updates that gave no useful information, further conversation was absent until they arrived in the prison's parking lot. Two uniformed police officers moved a barrier at the sight of the flashing blue and red strobes mounted around the car's headlights. They parked in a cluster of official-looking vehicles and climbed out of the car. They walked deliberately toward what looked like a gathering of the local brass.

One person wore a vest with SWAT on the back. Another was clad in formidable armor with AET stenciled on it for The Anti-Enhanced Threat agency. She recognized Paul Andrews among the others. He was from the Paranormal Defense Agency. She and Clement waited until the initial conversation broke up, then moved into the circle of people. She nodded. "Andrews. What do we have?"

The PDA agent replied, "Things on the inside seem to have reached a stasis point."

Clement asked, "Any word on Winston?"

He answered, "No information on anything specific other than a fire and a riot. Sounds like the prison staff has their hands full."

Cait replied, "You going in?"

The AET man said, "Two minutes. Waiting on override codes from Washington. I'm Eduardo Val, by the way."

"Cait Keane. Clement Austin. We're coming with you."

He shrugged, and she had the sense that in a different situation, he might argue the point. "Whatever. You're behind my team and with them." He gestured at Andrews and the woman beside him.

Andrews said, "This is Natalie Hood, my second in command. Let's get geared up."

Cait and Clement headed back to the car and popped open the trunk. She slipped on her bulletproof vest and checked to verify her pistol was loaded. Since the first fugitive hunt in Boston, she'd made it a practice to carry a magazine of anti-magic ammunition with her, which currently rode under her right armpit, along with another backup mag of standard ammo. Clement finished his preparations and grabbed a Colt M4 Carbine from the trunk. He asked if she wanted one, and Cait shook her head. "No, I think I have a better option."

She jogged over to the AET truck and said, "Hey, all. Cait Keane, deputy US marshal and part of the Special Operations Group. Can I borrow one of your rifles?"

A woman in AET armor detached a rifle from a wall-mounted rack and jumped down from the vehicle. "Have you used them before?"

Cait shook her head. "Trained with something similar a couple of years back, though."

The woman grinned and extended the weapon. "The selector chooses your fire mode. It won't shoot unless you've got a contact transponder." She reached into the truck and handed Cait a pair of gloves. "Pretty easy to use, although the beanbag shots have a bit of a recoil."

She nodded. "Thanks for the gear and the lesson. I promise not to make off with it afterward." The woman laughed, then the AET boss called for the assault team to get into position, and they moved.

Val's team led the way, rushing forward in ranks of two, rifles moving to cover all the angles as they advanced through the facility. Everyone they encountered was ordered to drop to the ground. If their targets didn't respond immediately, weapons went off, regardless of whether they were dressed as a guard, a worker, a prisoner, or anything else.

The AET's equipment was designed for maximum flexibility in order to adapt to whatever magical threat they might encounter. In this circumstance, they used a combination of beanbags from the under-barrel launchers and the electrical mode on the rifles. The weapons emitted a focused beam of electricity, like a wireless Taser, similar to what Cait did with her lightning. The attack was effective in bringing the opposition down quickly without permanently damaging them. When targets fell, the front lines would continue to advance while those behind secured them with zip ties. Those who did surrender were also bound, and the SWAT team trailing Cait, Clement, Andrews, and Hood took charge of them.

They passed through processing and entered the main area of the prison, which started with a large nexus of multiple wings. A battle still raged there, hands and fists, nightsticks and tasers. The guards carried no projectile weapons for fear that the prisoners would get their hands on them.

The AET troops fired indiscriminately and without warning, taking down guards and prisoners alike. Cait noted movement to her left and spotted a trio of people wearing guard uniforms coming her way down one of the corridors at a run. She shouted, "Stop and drop," but they continued forward, yelling something she couldn't make out. She pressed the button and pulled the trigger to fire a beanbag at the nearest. It caught him in his sternum, dropping him to the ground.

The other two advanced, undeterred, and she blasted them with the rifle's electrical attack, moving the beam from one to the other in a continuous discharge. They fell, and a SWAT team member moved in to tie them up.

Val called, "Heading for Solitary. Move it, people." She

raced along behind them as they sprinted down an empty corridor. Signs of past fighting were visible, but no enemies remained. When they reached the solitary wing, they discovered guards attempting to put out a fire the sprinkler system had not yet managed to overcome. The inferno appeared to be cascading outward from all the solitary cells, as if separate fires were trying to gather in the hallway. Her rifle dipped in frustration as she let out a low curse. Not only was there nothing left to fight, but she also couldn't imagine that anyone in the cells survived the inferno.

With their primary objective—taking possession of Winston—now impossible, Cait and Clement had returned to a guard post near the building's entrance when the AET team declared they had the situation under control. She called Sabrina and asked the infomancer if she had access to the prison's computer systems.

The response was what she expected. "Not at this time."

Cait replied, "What if I told you that the override code we used to get through the prison was 734921?"

"Stand by."

Clement said, "They won't like that."

She shrugged. "Sabrina's good. They won't know about it, and if they find out, I'll apologize. New kid on the block, doesn't understand the local rules, ordered her to do it." Her partner shook his head but didn't argue.

Sabrina reported, "Okay. I'm in. What do you need?"

Cait replied, "Evidence."

The infomancer laughed. "Vague much?"

Clement suggested, "Go back and see if you can discover anything notable that happened just before the riot report came in."

After several moments, Sabrina said, "All I can find is that the anti-magic emitters, both primary and secondary, that covered solitary confinement reported errors seventeen minutes before the fire alarms went off."

Cait asked, "Simultaneously?"

"Yeah."

Clement shook his head. "Sloppy. Inside job, you think?"

Cait frowned. "Seems too coincidental not to be, but I guess we can't take it as guaranteed."

Andrews arrived, and they shared the information with him. He didn't ask their source, for which she was grateful. He reported, "The place is locked down again, so we can turn our attention to figuring out what happened. Come with me."

He led them to a control room with an operator sitting at a bank of monitors, many small ones and a large display immediately in front of him. Andrews said, "All right, go back to seventeen minutes before the fire alarms went off and show me the areas where the anti-magic emitters for Solitary are." Two images that looked like separate storage closets came up on the main screen. "Now add the hallways outside them." The tech did, putting them on small displays near the primary one, but they showed nothing out of the ordinary.

"Let's rewind all of them at once and see what we can see." About seven minutes before the emitters went down, the cameras in the storage closets glitched. Immediately after in their scan, or just before the glitch in real-time, the ones outside in the hallway did, too. As they watched, the cameras flickered in sequence, covering the approach toward the anti-magic emitters.

Cait said, "That confirms it had to be a worker to have that kind of access to the space. Probably partnered with an infomancer to handle the cameras, I guess."

Andrews nodded. To the tech, he said, "You need to do a full search of your systems. Look for a hardware tap, too, something that would give an infomancer access from inside the prison."

Clement sighed. "And that leaves the fun part for you and me, partner." He sat down at a computer terminal and waved Cait over to sit beside him. "Give us permissions to the employee files over here. Time to start looking for our bad actor."

CHAPTER ELEVEN

Kono Zhelan, second in command of the Dragons after Yoshino Kyouka, drummed his fingers in the back of the car as it sped toward its destination. He had information to share and news that must be delivered in person out of both respect and practical necessity. He wore a blue pinstriped suit, a purple shirt, and a black tie, along with shiny black boots. His hair was a mop in the style of Korean boy bands, which, in combination with his ageless features, made him seem younger than he was. He had found this a benefit in his career more than once since others underestimated him because of it.

The car pulled to a halt outside a downtown hotel, and he opened the door himself rather than wait for his driver to do it for him. He strode through the lobby, raised a hand to discourage the concierge who moved to intercept him, and traveled in a straight line toward the bank of elevators at the far end. Only two of them rose to penthouse level, and he selected one of those, then waved a key fob at the detector once he was inside to confirm his permission to access the destination.

The doors opened onto an entry chamber with a single door opposite the lifts. A guard desk with override controls for the elevator was against the right-hand wall. Ahead of him stood two security guards, both of whom recognized him. He nodded, and they did the same. One gestured at the table that lay to the left.

Kono systematically pulled out his weapons, starting with the blades in his boots and moving up to the metal knuckles in one pocket and the switchblade in the other. He removed his belt and set it carefully on the table's surface, then opened his jacket so they could see his pistol. Using two fingers, he gingerly extracted it from its holster and deposited it on the table. Finally, he removed the beaded necklace from under his shirt, which, if needed, could be used as a garrote.

He then stepped forward and spread his arms. One bodyguard frisked him while the other waved a detection wand over him. When their review was completed, they offered him bows again, and the door was opened from the inside. Saito Iwaki, his superior's bodyguard, greeted him with a small inclination of his head. "Madame will see you in the main room."

Kono knew the way, having visited many times before, and walked briskly in that direction. When he entered the opulent space, he was, as always, struck by its beauty. Floor-to-ceiling windows covered two sides of the room, one showing the tops of the Boston skyline, the other looking out over the water. The furniture was entirely modern, as were the art prints on the walls, the metal frames that held them, and all the furniture. The floor appeared to be wooden planks, though it was likely some other material that would deaden sound more effectively. Without turning to face him, his host said, "Make yourself a drink."

He nodded and went to the bar set along a wall, dropped ice into a glass, and poured a liberal dose of vodka over it before adding tonic and a lime. "May I get you one?"

"No, thank you."

He moved to stand at her side and one pace behind as a sign of respect. She mused, "It's beautiful here at night." Her words held a note of wistfulness. "Of course, from this high up, one is insulated from the truth of life below." She turned to him, and her voice became businesslike. "Please, share your report."

The bluntness of the request surprised him since their meetings usually included sitting and making small talk before getting to the matter that had brought them together. "There has been a fire at the federal prison. It involved only the solitary confinement wing where the assassin was residing, to the best of our knowledge. We paid a guard to find a way to disable the anti-magic emitter as a prelude to portaling in and extracting our target. However, our insider didn't inform us of the time window in which the prison would be vulnerable, and he appears to have acted far faster than we expected, assuming the fire was magical in origin and not a random occurrence."

"The latter is unlikely." Her face was impassive, as was her voice. "Perhaps someone had the same idea we did."

Kono nodded. His mouth was dry. He wished he could take a sip from his drink, but he would not do so while speaking with Madame Yoshino. "It is possible. In either case, it was not us who acted at the prison, but nonetheless, action was taken."

"You believe it was Rosetta?"

He gave a single sharp nod. "That is a logical assumption."

She gestured at the couches, and he accepted the invitation. He moistened his mouth with his drink as she took her own seat and asked, "What do they have to gain?"

From the room's entrance, where he had watched unobtrusively, Saito replied, "Covering their tracks so we can't acquire proof they used the assassin to shift suspicion onto us."

Yoshino nodded slowly. "Possible. What else do we know?"

Kono answered, "Several fatalities, all of them burned beyond recognition. One is presumably Winston if he was indeed in Solitary as he was supposed to be."

Yoshino observed, "We need confirmation."

"Our infomancers penetrated the prison's systems. The authorities concluded that one of the bodies belongs to the assassin. It is unclear on what basis they made this determination."

She laughed darkly. "More corruption, most likely. We must discover the truth. See to it." She waved a hand, dismissing him.

Kono rose, bowed, and walked toward the corridor. At the door, Saito asked, "What is your plan?"

Because the bodyguard frequently spoke with Madame Yoshino's voice, he had to answer despite being her second in command. "First, I'll establish that our infomancers haven't discovered any more information. Second, I'll use our contacts within law enforcement to verify that what the infomancers are telling me is correct."

Saito nodded. "A wise precaution."

"Trust but confirm. Always a good practice. Beyond that, it seems as if the guard we paid to gain access to the prison is our most likely source of useful information, whether or not he was involved directly."

"Best move quickly before he, too, turns up as bones."

Kono walked into the hall and rearmed himself automatically. His thoughts were on the challenge of securing the guard. When he reached the car, he ordered the driver to take him to the nearest warehouse that served as headquarters for the Dragons' soldiers. He entered quietly, always appreciating the chance to observe his subordinates unobtrusively.

The room was active, full of people playing games, cleaning weapons, or sparring. When the first one spotted him and turned to face him at attention, a wave rippled outward, stilling other actions as everyone copied the first's motion. He nodded, pleased. After dealing with Madam Yoshino's bodyguard, it was nice to be treated appropriately for his station.

He announced, "We have a betrayer to hunt tonight, my friends. Prepare yourselves. We leave in fifteen minutes."

Kono headed to his personal chamber in the building. He had one in each of the Dragons' important bases, filled with duplicate equipment. A ten-digit code gave him access, and he stepped inside. He stripped off his suit, hanging it on a wooden hanger, then donned black pants and shirt along with light body armor. Two sheathed swords went into loops on the back of his armor, both positioned to be drawn over his right shoulder. He'd practiced the action so many times that the act of drawing and cutting was virtually instantaneous.

Next, he put on soft boots, which would give him excellent ground feel but also provide a modicum of protection against injury. Finally, he added a pistol and holster, attaching it to his belt and tying it around his thigh. He grabbed a black balaclava and carried it with him out into the main room to find his people ready. "Very well. Let's go capture a rat."

CHAPTER TWELVE

Once again, Cait was in the passenger seat while Clement was behind the wheel, this time speeding toward a house in the suburbs northeast of the city. Their review of employee records had revealed a guard who was supposed to be on shift had disappeared before the incident. They had delayed long enough to be positive he wasn't among those they'd knocked down on the way in and to gain at least a reasonable confirmation that one of the burned bodies wasn't him.

When those both came back negative, they'd taken off at a run. After a brief discussion, they'd decided to go it alone, rather than involving local authorities, for fear that their quarry would wind up spooked and run before they could secure him. As they took the exit from the highway that led to the guard's neighborhood, Clement killed the lights and siren. With their own sound and illumination gone, Cait thought the area was quieter and darker than expected. "Seems weird."

"Yeah. Let's get a better view before we get any closer."

Clement pulled to the curb and climbed out of the car. She joined him as he opened the trunk, and together they hauled out the heavy case containing the drone. They removed the cover, and a moment later, lights started to flicker on the device. It rose into the air, tilted left and right as if waving at them, and then flew off toward the house.

They stowed the container in the trunk and waited. Sabrina said, "Okay, the good news is there's a heat signal in the house. The bad news is it's not the only one. I'm reading a bunch of other heat signals all around the house."

She frowned. "Like, he's having a barbecue or something?"

"Only if the guests are sneaking in, based on movement patterns. I don't want to go low enough to switch to visual."

Clement observed, "Someone else is interested in our guard, I guess. That certainly makes his guilt more likely."

Cait replied, "Or we're all making the same mistake."

He retrieved a rifle and closed the trunk. "Doubtful."

She gestured at the house. "Yeah. Let's go see what we've got."

While they were still far enough away not to be seen or heard, Cait whispered the words to cast a veil of illusion over them. "I summon the glare of sun, the shadow of clouds, the silence of deepest night; in combination, concealment create." She drew her pistol, shifting it to her left hand, and held her right ready to summon additional magic. Sabrina's voice was a constant presence in their ears, guiding them along a path where the warm bodies surrounding the house would be least likely to detect them.

The infomancer stopped them suddenly, and Cait stared forward, trying to spot anything out of the ordinary. The infomancer said, "Thirty degrees right." She turned in that direction and saw a shadow move slightly, now able to identify it as a figure in black from head to toe that had shuffled forward a few feet.

She spoke as softly as she could, even though the veil dampened sound. "Anyone near him?"

"Negative."

"Okay. This one's mine. Austin, stay with me." She crept forward toward the target. When she judged she could no longer avoid notice, she extended the veil to cover him. A tremor of surprise ran through him, likely due to the magic's visual component, which slightly blurred the perception of the area beyond it. He didn't have time to do more than stiffen before Cait walked up behind him, pressed her fingertips to his head, and pushed electricity through them. The magical lightning shocked him into unconsciousness. She lowered him carefully to the ground and froze, waiting for a reaction that would signal they'd been detected.

Sabrina said, "Looks like you're good."

Cait frisked him, discovering a radio, a gun, and a short blade. She turned off the radio and clipped it on her belt, shoved the pistol in the back of her pants, and slipped the sheathed knife in her pocket. Her bulletproof vest made the process a little more challenging than it would've been without it, but she certainly wasn't going to leave him with any tools. She handcuffed him and muttered, "We should have brought more cuffs."

Clement chuckled quietly. "I'll add some more to the go bags when we get back."

Sabrina drew them back to the moment. "They're almost at the house."

Aza, flying above, said, "The house is encircled. Scream if you want me to attack."

Clement replied, "I guess stealth isn't going to do it. Morin, wake them up."

The drone emitted a bright light that moved over the ground as it flew. Loudspeakers blared, ordering everyone to disperse in a modulated version of Sabrina's voice. Cait heard both the infomancer's actual words and the replication of them almost simultaneously, which was weird enough that it momentarily captured her attention. She said, "If they turn to run, we'll try to sneak through them and get to the house."

But, unexpectedly, they didn't do so. Instead, pistols barked, and battle cries sounded as the group surrounding the house revealed itself to be two different groups that were demonstrably not allies. Cait frowned. "That was unexpected."

Clement replied, "Right?"

"While they're busy, let's go for the house." Having put the drone's broadcast in a loop, Sabrina again guided them through the heat signals as they moved toward the front door. When they reached it, Cait turned the handle but found it locked. She muttered, "We don't have time for this," and blasted the door off its hinges, sending it flying into the room. They rushed inside and she let the veil drop, then turned and slammed the pair of mysterious fighters that tried to follow them in back out through the doorway with another charge of magic. She slammed a wall of force in place to block it. "I need to stay close to keep this up. You search."

Clement nodded and moved deeper into the house. She stepped as far as she could away from the door while keeping it in sight and got a line on the back entrance as well. She conjured another force barrier in case someone got the clever idea of entering from that side of the structure. "What's going on, Morin?"

The infomancer replied, "They're still fighting outside. Doesn't look as if either has an advantage. One group appears to have mainly guns. The other one seems to be better at stealth."

"When this is over, we'll want to get the PD in here to take care of prisoners and injured. Ideally, we'd like to know who they are."

Sabrina replied, "You think it's someone other than the Dragons or the Roses?" Her voice held doubt.

"That's the most likely outcome, but we need confirmation. This is one weird town you've got here."

"You are correct," she said with a chuckle.

Clement came back into view, shaking his head. He said, "Morin, is he still in here?"

The infomancer replied, "With so many people around, the drone can't distinguish one from another, sorry."

Their quarry's whereabouts were revealed a moment later with a huge crashing sound. Cait immediately realized what it was and dispelled the force shield on the front entrance, running outside in time to see a large pickup truck with oversized tires barrel onto the street from the driveway, pieces of the ruined garage door falling off as it sped away.

Her head snapped around to the right as she caught the motion of a figure raising a pistol toward her, and she blasted him with enough force magic to send him hurtling backward through the air. *Okay, Cait, take it down a notch.*

Clement said, "First one to the car gets to drive," and took off at a run.

CHAPTER THIRTEEN

Clement outraced her to the car, although Cait could've taken him by using magic to speed up. She didn't think he would've come through on the bet and allowed her to drive, so it hadn't been worth the effort. The vehicle lurched into motion as soon as her backside hit her seat, and she slammed the door and scrabbled for the seatbelt. "You're a crazy person. You know that?"

Clement, his gaze fixed on the road in front of him, replied, "It's been said." He activated the sirens, the flashing lights, and the high beams. "Give me a vector, Morin."

The infomancer advised, "Take a left, go two blocks, and make a right. It looks like he's headed out of town."

Cait said, "Just as well. A car chase in the shopping district would be a bad idea."

Clement ordered, "Have the PD isolate the route so no one can get onto it and cover the exits in case he decides to take one before we reach him. We'll handle the takedown, but if they can do all that and still get spike strips deployed in time to intercept him, that would be a useful move."

Sabrina replied, "Affirmative."

Except when he was taking a curve, which he did at speeds she wouldn't have dared, Clement pushed the car as hard as it would go. After several minutes, they could make out the taillights of the pickup truck in the distance. The car's display showed a map with their position and the truck's on it, although their target's location was getting fuzzier as the drone fell farther behind. They were both so focused on the view ahead that when the additional cars joined the chase from the sides and rear, moving even faster than the Charger, it came as a surprise.

Four had appeared: two of them ahead, closer to the fleeing guard, and a pair behind, accelerating toward their vehicle. Metallic pings signaled the impacts of bullets on the car. Clement swore and barked, "This would be a good time for you to do something."

Cait rolled down her window and pulled herself out to sit on the doorframe, turned toward the rear of their car, positioning a wall of force in front of her. Bullets slammed into the outer edges of it; they would have missed her anyway, but the barrier stopped them. *Now to get rid of them before they think to switch to anti-magic rounds if they have them.*

She targeted the car coming up on that side behind them and fired. She aimed at the front tire, knowing her rounds were too small a caliber to do serious damage to the engine unless she got a lucky shot. Her bullets struck true and the tire popped, sending the car into a skid. The driver overcorrected, and the vehicle tumbled, sliding down the road on its roof in a shower of sparks.

When Clement yelled, "Hold on," she threw a band of

force across to the far side of the car and gripped it tightly. He tapped the brakes, then wrenched his wheel sideways, slamming the back left of the Charger into the front right of the pursuing car. The impact spun the trailing vehicle, and it was quickly left behind.

Aza flew down, and she called, "You get the one up there on the left. I'll get the one on my side. It doesn't matter if people are inside. Take it out."

The dragon roared and replied, *Consider them gone*, before flying into the air. She lost sight of him as she focused on her own task. She holstered her pistol and climbed onto the roof of the car. Clement was going at maximum speed, but they were only closing on the other vehicles slowly. *At the rate I'm winding up on top of cars, I should get myself a pair of those sci-fi magnetic boots or something.*

With that option currently unavailable, Cait could only trust her balance and keep herself ready to add more shields if she was suddenly dislodged from the car. She calculated the trajectory to the vehicle ahead on the right, which was too far for her magical jump to bridge the distance or for her to be accurate with her pistol. Fortunately, she had a lifetime of training in targeting her magical attacks.

She considered fire but feared it would damage the pickup truck. Force presented a similar problem since she worried the car might spin directly into their quarry if struck. Her best hope was to take out both back tires simultaneously, and the only spell she had that could potentially accomplish that was lightning. She envisioned a barrier between her target and the pickup and cast force magic to bring it into reality. It wouldn't be strong enough to keep the two cars from colliding if that was the outcome of her attack, but it would prevent the electricity from spilling over.

She concentrated on maintaining the first magic while she gathered her power, then sent it out in a wave of sparking forks of lightning to caress the tail of the enemy's car. It took a few seconds, during which she wondered what the people in the car might be thinking, before the two back tires blew and the car dropped down onto its rims. The loss of speed created by the drag immediately removed that car from the chase, and they flashed by it. She turned to watch as it wound up veering off into the grass on the side. Her attention returned to the road ahead at the perfect moment to watch Aza's attack.

She'd imagined the dragon might break windows with his talons or use fire to knock out the car. She hadn't expected that he would return to the size he'd been when she'd met him—about the same as a large horse—and crash down on the roof from above, crushing the passenger compartment. He launched back into the air as the car careened off the road.

Cait climbed back into the car, secured her seatbelt, and ran fingers through her tangled hair, trying to get it out of her face. Clement said, "A dragon just dive-bombed that car, right? That's what I saw?"

"Yep. Unpredictable, that one. Probably because he's young, but he's a dragon, so who knows?" They continued to slowly narrow the distance to the pickup truck. The drone had been outraced, and Clement had switched the car's display to a map and zoomed it out so they could see what was going to happen. She pointed. "Looks like a dead-end road ahead. Wonder if we can force him onto it?"

Clement replied, "Can you ask your dragon?"

"Unfortunately, no."

"Okay. Hang on." He flipped open a panel she'd taken for part of the car's internal decoration. Underneath it lay two switches and two buttons.

She asked, "You have a spy car?"

Clement laughed. "I have the *beginnings* of a spy car. Only one of those is wired up. Here's hoping I still have a spy car in a few seconds, and we're not red paste on the windshield." Before she could ask him what that meant, he flicked the top toggle.

The car shot forward, the speedometer jerking to the right as whatever he'd done gave the Charger a speed boost, slamming her back into her seat. He shouted, "Nitro." They drew even with the truck, then got ahead of it. He pulled into the middle of the road, and when the moment was right, he slammed on the brakes.

Cait jerked forward against her harness, the breath leaving her lungs. The maneuver worked. Their quarry's reflexive response caused him to turn and barrel off onto the side road to avoid hitting them. When they came to a stop, Clement breathed for a second before throwing the car into reverse and stomping on the accelerator. A minute and a half later, they had the pickup in sight again. She looked at the map and said, "I don't think we want to let him get to the end. He might wreck."

Clement growled, "You have a better idea?"

"Not sure it's better, but it's an idea." She lowered her window and sat on the edge again, waving at Aza above.

He came down to fly beside the car, and she shouted, "Force the other truck onto the grass." Fortunately, both sides of the road were covered by fields, uneven terrain that would be no fun to drive over but would be safer than ramming head-on into whatever waited to give the moniker "dead-end" to the road.

She climbed back into the car, buckled her belt, and leaned forward to watch. Aza flew in an arc, then made an attack run on the road, starting his fire breath early enough to provide the guard a chance to react. He did the only thing he could to avoid the flames, which was to peel off into the grass to the right.

Unfortunately—for him at least—he lost control as his tires met the unpredictable surface. The car hit a low rise and flipped several times, coming to a rest with its wheels on the ground. Clement hit the brakes, and Cait climbed out of the car and launched at the pickup. The guard was inside, his head bleeding from where it had struck the side door. He was barely conscious. His limbs were moving, so she didn't fear a neck or back injury.

Clement arrived and helped her pry the bent and dented door open and pull the guard out of the truck. As she opened the portal to the hospital, she observed, "Getting tired of being a magical ambulance."

Her colleague laughed. "You break 'em, you deliver 'em. Seems fair to me."

CHAPTER FOURTEEN

The next morning, Cait ran up the stairs from the subway and found Clement waiting for her at the top, just like he said he would be. He grinned. "Made it to the middle of the week without getting killed. Not bad."

She shook her head with a smile. "Setting a pretty low bar, my friend. How's the car?"

He scowled. "Dropped her off at the shop this morning. Being repaired. They estimate five days. Apparently, mixing Nitro boost and hard braking is a rotten idea."

She winced. "Sorry."

"It's the job. Besides, the chief is normally willing to reimburse me a little."

"That's good. So, where *is* this place?"

He gestured down the block, and they started walking. "The Paranormal Defense Agency office is in the local government building. Not sure why, since they're not technically local."

She looked ahead at the imposing structure, still a

distance away. "Real estate is probably at a premium around here, yes?"

He nodded. "Especially in the city. Not as bad in some of the suburbs, although the closer you are to downtown the less available it is, so it costs more. The same as everywhere. Don't get me started on the number of people who buy property only to rent it out."

They arrived at the building and passed through the entrance security screening after showing their credentials. Elevators delivered them to the fifteenth-floor office of the PDA, Boston Division. *Bureau? Unit? How about "Boston Bunch?"* A receptionist dressed in an inexpensive-looking suit and wearing scuffed shoes escorted them into the conference room. He said, "You're the first to arrive. The others will be in shortly. There's coffee in the carafe on the credenza."

They offered their thanks as he departed. Once the door closed behind him, Clement asked, "What do you think? He's like, twelve?"

She laughed. "Fourteen, at least. Either way, it's clear they start them off young in the Paranormal Defense Agency."

The others filed in, including Chief Levitt, as well as people she recognized from the prison: Eduardo Val, Paul Andrews, and Natalie Hood. When everyone was seated and properly beveraged, Andrews began, "Thank you all for coming. Let's get started. First, I just received an update reporting that we've got a preponderance of evidence that one of the bodies in the fire was Winston."

Simon replied, "What evidence?"

"Given the burning, it's mainly a judgment on size,

that's true. But the cameras didn't see him leaving after he was locked in, including the one in his cell."

Clement asked, "So, someone saw him burn on video?"

Andrews' face twisted at the question, which was valid but harsh, in her opinion. "No. The heat killed the feed before the fire got to him."

Wonder if he's uncomfortable with the burning or if he isn't so certain? She said, "So, it's unlikely but possible that he might've made it out."

Andrews gave a brief nod. "I would say *highly* unlikely." He paused, waiting for a reply, then asked, "Anything else on that topic?"

When no one responded, his second in command set a small device on the table. It was rectangular, about the size of a deck of playing cards. "We found this beside one of the deactivated anti-magic emitters. Our best guess is whoever put it there believed the fire would destroy it, or you would think they'd have put a destruct on it so we wouldn't find it afterward."

Val asked, "What is it?"

Hood shrugged. "It's a magical device, for sure. We're not positive about its purpose, though."

Thinking of Aisling, Cait asked, "Can I have it to show to an expert, or at least have some pictures of it?"

The other woman nodded. "Pictures, sure. I'll send our analysis over to you. The device stays with us for the time being, though."

"So, does this mean that whoever did this has technomancers in their organization?"

Val replied, "They could. I know if I was in charge, I

would want to. But it also might have come from the Purple Market."

Cait frowned. "The what?"

The AET lead explained, "That's what the underground exchange for magical and technomagical items is called here. Because of the color of the magic crystals."

"I didn't realize Boston had one. I've only heard of them in New York, LA, and Dallas. In Columbus, we had some independent practitioners but not a market as such."

Andrews replied, "Almost every city has one, although most are much smaller and more informal than the cities Eduardo mentioned. Columbus does too, but it's quite inactive."

Simon asked, "Do either of you have someone inside it?"

Val replied, "Investigation's not really our thing," and looked at Andrews.

The head of the PDA added, "We don't have anyone inside, either. It's heavily tied to the criminal environment as near as we've been able to tell, which adds weight to the idea that it could have been the source of this material."

The rest of the meeting amounted to very little, and Cait was glad when it finished. Once they'd made it outside, Clement said, "I'm going to go back to the office and talk to Sabrina, find out what she can dig up about the Purple Market. I don't think we've had much interaction with it in the past."

Simon replied, "Not during my time here, that's for sure. I'll go with you. Keane, how about you gather up Bradley and go see what you can force out of the guard you captured."

"Happy to."

After meeting back at the Moakley, she and Garrett stopped for lunch at a small storefront that served a wide variety of hot dogs. She selected the Hawaiian, with bacon and pineapple, and a Chicago dog topped in the traditional style. Both were amazing, and when she was done, she wanted more. She finished her soda as they walked through security at the hospital and tossed the empty cup into the nearest bin.

Walking over to the information desk, she flashed her badge and asked where their prisoner was. An elevator took them to the twelfth floor again, and they were stopped by a blue-uniformed policeman as they stepped off. They presented their credentials, then repeated the process at a second checkpoint manned by plainclothes officers before being permitted access to the secure wing.

The room wasn't as nice as the one the assassin had occupied, with a smaller TV and lacking the abundant built-in equipment, the guest chair, and the lawyer. The prison guard sat upright in bed with a bandage adorning the left side of his head, but otherwise, he looked alert and mostly hale. He was watching a court show on television with a scowl. Garrett quipped, "Studying up for your appearance?"

He looked around, and his frown deepened. "Cops?"

Cait shook her head. "Marshals. One of the murders you assisted in was a witness of ours."

He leaned back with a groan. "I wasn't told there would

be violence. They were just supposed to break someone out of Solitary."

Garrett replied, "And you assumed they wanted to invite him over for a party or something?"

The man shrugged. "Guess I was in denial. Or, what's it called? 'Temporary insanity.'"

Cait chuckled darkly. "More like permanent stupidity. No one's gonna buy any of those excuses, Wallace." She found a picture of the technomagical device on her phone and showed it to him. "Were you the one who installed this?"

He nodded. "Yeah. Near an emitter. That's where they wanted it."

Garrett asked, "Where did you get it?"

"It was left for me at a neutral location. I don't know where it came from before that."

Cait replied, "What's it do?"

"I can't be positive since I'm not a magical or whatever, but they talked about it like it was their way into the prison. Gave out a signal that told them where to go."

Garrett stepped closer so he could stare down at the man. "So, who was it? Dragons? Roses? Someone else?"

He shook his head. "I tell you that, I'm dead."

Cait sighed. "Those folks have already killed a judge and started a fire in a federal prison, killing several more people. You *really* think they're going to let you, a loose end, live?"

Wallace groaned. "I was just trying to make a little extra cash, you know?"

Garrett pressed, "Extra cash from who?"

"Both of them. I alerted my contact, who said he was

from the Roses. I was planning to inform the others, too, but they acted too quickly. I never got to the point of figuring out how it would work with the Dragons."

Cait asked, "So, you're sure it was Rosetta's people?"

He shrugged. "Assuming he wasn't lying. Yeah, that's always the problem, isn't it? You just can't trust criminals not to lie."

"Okay. Stay safe, heal up. As soon as you're good to go, we'll move you into protective custody." She walked out the door and made a beeline for the plainclothes officers. "Keep an extra special eye on this one. We'll need him in court. He's gotten us one step closer to the people who did this."

CHAPTER FIFTEEN

After learning about the Purple Market, the idea that she needed to know more about it wouldn't leave her head for the rest of the day. That continued into the evening, and it was still on her mind the next morning. When she arrived at work, she made sure nothing critical was waiting in her inbox and went over to Sabrina's workspace. In quiet tones, she asked, "What were you able to find out about the Purple Market?"

The infomancer gestured for Cait to take the seat beside her desk. Its surface was bare except for a single tablet that was perfectly centered and a large computer monitor. "Well, it exists. It's not a geographical location like the fish market. It's a bunch of places that are only connected because they all traffic in magical items and services."

"Like what?"

Sabrina shrugged. "From what the infomancer boards on the magical dark web share, just about anything you need. Either they'll have it or have the contacts to get it."

Cait frowned. "Sounds dangerous."

"That's my read on it. I have the impression they're very careful who they let interact with them."

"Were you able to find any agency with an informant inside?"

The other woman shook her head. "I put out the word among the government infomancers I trust. No one had anything useful."

Cait scowled. "And we definitely don't want to go beyond those you trust for fear of alerting them that we're looking into them."

"Because of the danger, yes."

"I wonder what it would take to get in there?"

Sabrina's reply was slow and regretful. "The official records where it's been mentioned cover the gamut of criminal enterprises. The single thing they seem to have in common is that they're not newbs."

Cait leaned forward. "Inexperienced, you mean?"

"Yeah. Gaming term."

"I haven't forgotten about watching one of your tournaments when things slow down." She tapped a red-painted fingernail against her teeth. "All right. Let's say I wanted to wander in and take a look. What would we have to do to make that happen?"

Sabrina smiled. "First, we need to go get some coffee. Then we need to visit the dungeon."

Thirty minutes later, after walking in the sun with their coffee for a bit, they entered Sabrina's workspace. The infomancer changed into her hacking clothes—black leggings and t-shirt and boots—and sat down at her computers. Cait was ensconced on one end of the comfy couch. Sabrina said, "We're going to set up a false identity for you. I think the easiest criminal to spoof would be a burglar, someone who breaks into rich people's homes to steal stuff. That would give you a plausible reason to need magic and magical technology."

Cait nodded. "Okay. I've always wanted to be Catwoman."

"Seriously, who hasn't?" Sabrina's fingers danced on the keyboard, a pleasant clickety-clack in Cait's ears, and a series of images appeared on the display. She gestured. "Which picture do you like best?"

They were all images of her. "First, creepy."

The other woman laughed. "It's locally archived surveillance footage. I have access to whatever images the system has until it overwrites them."

She lifted an eyebrow. "Okay, two percent less creepy." Sabrina chuckled, and Cait chose one. It grew to fill the monitor.

"Hair color?"

"I can change that magically. Let's go with blonde."

Sabrina hit some buttons, and the hue shifted. "Like that?"

Cait regarded it with a frown of concentration. "A little whiter." After a moment, it was the way she wanted it.

The infomancer said, "Okay, I can manipulate your face electronically however you want. What can you do with makeup?"

"The only thing I'm good at is making myself look more

angular. Everything else I try leaves me looking like a punk rocker from the nineteen-eighties."

Sabrina laughed and made a few changes. "How's that?"

I wish I was that attractive in real life. "Excellent."

"All right. I'm going to assign you new fingerprints. They'll print out on the 3-D printer over there. You'll have to cut them out and glue them on, but they should be sufficient unless someone tries to pry them off."

She replied, "I hope it's a strong glue."

"It'll be fine. Now, let's see—story time. I think you started out in Hartford." Over the next half-hour, they filled in the details of the fictional thief's background, including stints in prison and items she'd allegedly stolen that had histories in the Boston black market. Finally, obviously satisfied, Sabrina said, "All right. That's as good as we're going to get. What name would you like, and where do you want to put the records?"

Cait had been thinking about those questions the whole time. "Lexi Matthews. Let's assume that the Boston PD is compromised. Drop it in there. Afterward, I guess Hartford, too, if there's any record of me having been imprisoned there."

Sabrina nodded. "Okay. Time to put on the VR." Cait complied, and Sabrina's loading construct appeared. "They've got some decent infomancers, but I've done a lot of research on this system, along with most of the other important ones in Boston."

Cait interrupted, "Including the PDA?"

The other woman laughed. When she was in her element, the awkward edge she either possessed or affected vanished, and the sound was almost sultry. "What a naughty question to ask. But yes, of course."

"Good to know."

"Here we go." They materialized on a rocky beach, with dirty sand, scraggly grass, and rocks all around.

"Where are we?"

Sabrina replied, "Alcatraz."

In her best Sean Connery imitation, Cait replied, "Welcome to the Rock."

The infomancer gave a soft snort. "Really more *Escape from Alcatraz*, but I'll accept your answer. You know, there are fan theories that Sean Connery is actually playing the character of James Bond in *The Rock*."

"No way."

Sabrina's voice sounded pleased as she replied, "Yep. Look it up. There's a lot of evidence." Her avatar started to move, climbing up the hill, staying low. It was daytime, and momentarily Cait thought they should've waited for night. Then she gave herself a mental slap on the side of the head. *It's a simulation. It would only have night if they wanted it to have night. And why would they want it to have night?*

When they reached the top of the rise, the main prison loomed on a diagonal to the right, and they moved away from it. Cait remarked on that, and Sabrina said, "Just like in both movies, trying to get in or out of the prison over the walls doesn't make sense, so we're going in through the mechanical systems."

Cait understood enough about infomancy to know their route was a metaphor for the programs Sabrina was launching against the defenses the police had put into place. Nonetheless, it felt tense, like they were there. "Can I do more than just ride along?"

Sabrina picked the lock of an outbuilding and swung the door open, then led Cait inside. The infomancer replied, "Not with current technology. Military researchers are working on how to do it using, ironically, a techno-magical interface, but I don't think it'll work out. Too many conversions. Computers to magic, to thought, back to magic, back to computer. Takes too much time, even at the fastest throughput."

She pried a grate off the floor and lowered herself into a wet pipe just large enough to crawl into. Sabrina explained, "Storm outflow. Part of the modeling of the original facility. Not sure why they preserved it, although alarms are plentiful along the way, so they might've just wanted to offer an obvious way in."

Cait asked, "If it's obvious, why are we taking it?"

"A, because it's the best route, and B, because my ability to defeat their alarms is much stronger than their ability to set them."

They made their way through scenes she remembered from *The Rock* and others she vaguely recalled from the Clint Eastwood prison movie, including rolling through jets of fire that activated on a timer. Finally, they climbed up and out through a hole in the wall into a cell. When they were inside, Cait turned and saw that a poster of Rita Hayworth hung on the wall over the entrance they'd just come through. She shook her head. "*Shawshank*. You're a solid movie fan, aren't you?"

Sabrina replied, "Yes. Gives my brain some downtime."

Cait replied, "Me too. Maybe we can get together to watch some when things slow down a bit?"

Sabrina's voice held a smile when she said, "I'd love that." She moved toward the bars and added, "And here we go." She reached into a pouch attached to her belt, pulled out a piece of paper, folded it into an airplane, and sent it flying through the bars. It didn't soar like a normal one but darted to the middle of the space, curved to the right, and then shot down at a diagonal.

A couple of moments later, Sabrina said, "It's in. Time to go."

With a sudden glow, the surrounding image melted, leaving her back in the waiting room for the system. She removed the virtual reality headset, blinking. "So, it's all good?"

Sabrina spun in her chair and nodded. "Yep. Lexi is now as real as we can make her. Try not to get yourself arrested since we'd have a lot of explaining to do."

Cait laughed. "I'll do my best."

CHAPTER SIXTEEN

That night, Cait sat in front of her mirror, staring at the woman reflected in it. "Time to become someone else." She focused on her hair and whispered an illusion spell she and her sisters had used since they were children for entertainment. "Red to blonde to black to brown." After so much time, the rest of the words had fallen away, and all she needed was the first part to trigger her intention. Beginning at the roots and spreading out to the tips, her lustrous red hair became the white blonde of the Lexi Matthews persona Sabrina had created.

She spent some time with her makeup, using rouge and lighteners together to make her face appear more angular. It would hold up against reasonable investigation, and if questioned, she could always claim to have done the same cosmetics for the photo, as well. Finally, she opened the case holding the false fingerprints and used a small pot of glue Sabrina had given her to secure each to her fingertips. She turned to Aza, who was lying on the bed. "How's it look?"

He yawned and replied, "Like you with blonde hair and obvious makeup."

"You're no help, you know that?" He chuffed a laugh as she rose and crossed to the drawers that held her clothes. She pulled out a pair of leather pants she'd worn on infrequent nights out in Columbus, along with matching boots, both appropriate for a nightclub, and a bold red blouse that was stark against her pale skin.

The outfit offered no room to hide weapons other than blades in the boots. They weren't designed for it, so she slipped the pair of switchblades she owned into the sides, then laced the footwear up tightly enough that they wouldn't betray her but loose enough that she could get at the knives. *I can deal with the discomfort. And I don't need any other weapons. I've got my magic.* Her bracelet was hidden amongst several others, all of them more ostentatious, as it was conceivable that it could be recognized. She'd also turned it, so the turquoise faced backward. Still, it made her slightly nervous to know it was visible at all. *I need to find something specific to cover it in the future if I'm going to continue doing stupid stuff like this.*

A thought occurred to her, and she sighed. "I just realized I can't wear the dragon necklace tonight. It's possible someone has seen Cait wear it."

"You're wearing your bracelet," Aza countered logically.

"Yeah, but it's disguised by the others. I don't have any jewelry I can use to hide something as unique as your necklace form. You'll have to stay outside and watch my back."

He bounded off the bed to stand beside her, as tall as

her upper thigh. "That's acceptable as long as you promise to run if there's trouble."

She chuckled. "You know it. Getting into any situation while working under a false persona is a bad, bad idea."

Sabrina's research on the infomancer message boards had identified a potential starting point for where to find the Purple Market. They both believed more specific information could be had with a little work, but it would make sense for her assumed identity to have to figure it out rather than leaping ahead to the last step in the chain.

After a brief subway ride, Cait's alter ego walked into the Newbury hotel, a luxury brand on the south side of the city, and took a seat at the bar. The clientele was upscale, and her outfit was a little off amongst the more fashionable people filling the space. Every man wore a suit, and most of the women had on dresses suitable for fancy parties.

Aza said in her mind, "If you need anything, just scream." The knowledge that he was outside perched on a nearby building and ready to assist was a good feeling. After finishing her first cocktail, an old-fashioned that was a little stronger than she was accustomed to, she asked the bartender if he knew of where she could get a "Magic Flame" shot. He laughed and replied, "Any corner, I'm guessing."

She shook her head as he returned with her second drink. "No, I don't want the fake stuff. I want the real magical version. I have a, uh, *friend* who's a connoisseur."

He raised an eyebrow. She knew the difference between the real magical version of the aphrodisiac and that "sold on the corners," as he put it, so she was not ordinary. The reference to a friend suggested she was an escort, an erroneous assumption her outfit didn't counter. He asked, "You're sure?"

She nodded. "Definitely. I need the real thing."

"Can't help you. Sorry." The way he said it told her it wasn't an honest rejection. Sure enough, after she paid the bill and added a fifty-dollar tip, he slid a glass of seltzer in front of her and placed a napkin beside it. The napkin had the address of a nightclub written on it, alongside a strange squiggly line with a star at the end of it. She looked up the destination on her phone, discovering it was across town. She summoned a car, then stepped outside as it pulled up. A glance up at Aza's perch confirmed he was watching. *All right. Onward we go.*

When she arrived at the nightclub, she had to wait in line at the door for twenty minutes before she could get in. She considered trying to tip the bouncers, but the fifty she'd bestowed upon the bartender was not a small sacrifice, given her pay grade. Following the path drawn on the napkin and judging that the sharp diagonal line meant to go upstairs, she found her way to a second-floor bar.

A woman in a white shirt and glittering blue vest was behind it, serving drinks quickly and efficiently to the throngs of people awaiting them. The nightclub was also rather upscale, though not as much as the hotel bar. Cait mentioned the magical drug to the bartender and got a raised eyebrow in return. She slipped over another fifty with a concealed wince and said, "I'm just looking for a lead. It won't come back to you."

As the other server had, the woman said no. But before Cait departed, she'd received another napkin with an address written on it. She headed back outside into the darkness as the old day ticked over to the new and grumbled, "This is not my idea of a fun night on the town." Her new destination was twenty-some blocks away, and she had no desire to walk it, so she summoned another car.

At the next place, she instructed the car to go past the address for another couple of blocks before she got out. Then she walked into an alley and used magic to send herself up to the roof of a building across the street from her target. Aza landed beside her, and she crouched to examine the place she'd been sent. A sign on the front proclaimed, Games of Chance. The venue's name was Abstention, which seemed like an odd choice, given what it was.

Equally strange was the business' clientele, judging by those she saw entering during the next hour. Some were obviously wealthy and would've fit in well at the first bar. Others were more like the nightclub's patrons, younger, tipsier, louder. Several, though, appeared to her to be far too young to have the disposable income for gambling. She suggested, "Maybe they're the video gamers."

Aza replied, "Or maybe they're infomancers, or Purple Market people, or employees. You won't figure it out from here, that's for sure."

She sighed. "I was hoping to connect with the underground without having to pay for it, other than the few tips I've already passed out. But if this is the place, that's not an option. I'll need a gambling stake if I go in there. I can't pretend to be visiting for the video games, given my lack of skill."

He laughed. "You could bring Sabrina."

"No, too dangerous for that. Too many unknowns."

"Marshals give you money?"

She shook her head. "Doubt it. Infiltration like this isn't really something the marshals do. But I have a source of funds. One that'll probably add credibility to my cover." She rose and rubbed at her tired eyes. "But I can't access it until tomorrow. So, time to go home and get some sleep."

CHAPTER SEVENTEEN

F riday morning was filled with important meetings, requiring Cait to be back in her proper hair, makeup, and sharply styled business suit, with Aza around her neck. It started with a discussion between the marshals and building security for the Moakley, trying to identify how the devices discovered during their sweep—several of them that were identical to the one they'd found in Judge Meyer's chambers—could have gotten there.

That led to a bout of territorial defensiveness that occupied too much of the meeting before they agreed to review the employee files together. Her office's concession was that it would include *all* employees, including the marshals. She thought that was petty but also a small and inoffensive price to pay.

When that was complete, she had a one-on-one with Chief Levitt. They talked about her time at the office so far, discussed the Special Operations Group (SOG) in greater detail, and then agreed she was doing a fine job and should keep doing so while keeping the lines of communication between them wide open.

After that, she took her phone into the conference room and participated in a videoconference with the SOG, a monthly update that discussed general procedural details before progressing into an animated conversation about what their annual extended training should cover this year. Her opinion was that they needed more expertise in stealth incursions. Based on the early discussion, though, it seemed like aerial deployment operations might wind up being the winner. *That's fine. It's not like I'm too good to need practice at that, either.*

Finally, noon arrived, and she readied herself to head out to the bank to get what she needed for the night's adventure. Sabrina stopped her and asked, "Are you still looking for an apartment?"

Cait replied, "Yeah, actually." While that task never completely left her mind, it also kept getting pushed into the back.

The infomancer smiled. "I've got a line on a great one for you. Word of mouth, not officially on the market. You want to come take a look? It's not far by subway, so it shouldn't take much time."

She suppressed a reflexive frown at the potential change of plans. "As long as there's time to get to the bank afterward."

"The chief is taking a half-day, and last I checked, we don't have a time clock. Plus, we wind up working weekends off the clock. If lunch goes a little long, no one's going to fire us."

Cait laughed. "Well, when you put it that way, sure. I'd love to."

They took the subway in the basement of the building through a half-dozen stops, then walked out into a neighborhood filled with industrial-looking buildings. Sabrina gestured at one diagonally across the street. "It used to be a grain-processing factory. When it went out of business, it was empty for a while before a developer turned it into a bunch of separate apartments. The one we're interested in is in the tall section off to the left."

The nearest structure appeared to have been divided into three individual sections, two of them tall, the other only a couple of stories high. Sabrina typed a code on the keypad next to the door, and it unlocked. She explained, "I live on the sixth floor. The opening is on the seventh, but it's the same owner."

Cait nodded and followed her into an old-style metal cage elevator, which Sabrina hauled closed behind her. As it shuddered and shook its way up the floors, she said, "This seems like an exclusive place."

The infomancer chuckled. "You could say that. Maybe not at first, but it's become one over time. Generally, people invite their friends to move in. Or coworkers," she added quickly.

They got off on the seventh floor, and Sabrina typed in a different code on another door. It opened to reveal a loft-style space with no internal room divisions other than those sectioning off the bathroom and shower. The ceiling was higher than usual, about a story and a half, she guessed, and the walls held lots of windows through which sunlight slanted in. The floors were well-polished hardwood, and large fans spun overhead. It wasn't the biggest apartment she'd ever seen, although it was larger than any she'd lived in. *It's also way better than my hotel room.* She said, "It's gorgeous. I'm not sure I can afford this much space in the city, though."

Sabrina replied, "I didn't want to mention this part until you saw it. We're all members of a co-op that owns these two floors, plus another two higher up. We only charge what's needed to service the mortgage. In return for lower rent, everyone helps everyone else. And you can only join by referral."

Cait gave a slight frown. "How could I help?"

The other shrugged. "Maintaining the place, for a start. We all do some cleaning regularly and help prepare places for showing when someone moves out. Some improvements here and there, according to your skills. It's kind of fun. We normally turn it into a party. Also, maybe magical stuff." Her voice lowered. "I don't know what people need, but I'm sure you can find a way to do your part."

"How does that work?"

Sabrina replied, "Occupancy is in three-month increments. At the end of that time, everyone is reviewed to verify they're contributing at what the community deems an appropriate level. If you are, great. If not, you have three more months to make it better. We rarely, if ever, have someone who doesn't get with the program by the end of their first six-month period and stay that way after."

From around her neck, Aza said, *I like it. I'll have to pull back my claws so I don't scratch up the floors.*

She smothered a laugh. "Is it pet-friendly?"

Sabrina nodded. "Yes. Even for dragons."

Cait sighed. She seriously liked it and was already having visions of what it would be like to live there. She was afraid to ask the next question, but she had to. "How much?" Sabrina named a number. "Really?"

The infomancer replied, "Really-really."

"Well, then, when can I move in?"

The other woman smiled. "Today, if you want. But whenever. Should I let the others know you're in?"

Cait nodded and grinned widely. "Definitely." She grabbed Sabrina in a sudden hug, and the one she got in return was fiercer than she could've expected.

Her new neighbor said, "You owe me a movie night."

Cait laughed. "A debt I will be more than happy to pay."

She separated from Sabrina when they reached the office and headed to the bank. She identified herself to the staff and was escorted into the vault, where she opened her safe deposit box. Inside was a bundle of cash, several thousand dollars that constituted her emergency fund. The container also held a pouch filled with gemstones and other small objects from Oriceran, rare and valuable items her father had found on his various explorations. He'd given some to each of his daughters, and she had kept hers at hand, against what need she didn't know. "But now, I do," she muttered.

Aza replied, "They're beautiful."

She nodded and selected two, each of which was worth almost a thousand dollars. "More importantly, they're valuable. Now we need to find somewhere to sell them."

She went back to the office and discussed it with Sabrina, who did some research and found a pawnshop that was suspected of buying stolen items. It was just what she needed, the sort of place her new identity would frequent to get rid of the less valuable items she acquired on the job.

She returned to the hotel after work and enjoyed the surge of happiness that accompanied the realization she wouldn't be staying there much longer. "We can start moving stuff over the weekend or during the evenings next week. It should only take a few days to get enough that we can stay there."

Aza leapt on the bed, bouncing several times. "We have to get a great big bouncy bed."

She laughed. "Okay, buddy. I think we can manage that."

"And a huge television. Much larger than this one."

"Now you're getting into expensive goods. We'll also need some furniture, kitchen stuff, and so forth. Maybe dial it back a bit. I'm not made of money."

He ignored her. "And a giant fish tank like the ones I've seen on TV, filled with colorful fish."

She shook her head with a chuckle. "Keep dreaming, dragon." She changed into her disguise and headed out, again taking a car and exiting it a couple of blocks away from her target. Aza was on the roof of the building as she entered the pawnshop, which was typical of its kind. Random items sat on tables or hung on the walls with prominent price tags, most of which seemed excessive for the objects they were attached to. The cashier's cage was in the back, forcing one to experience the whole shop before reaching it. A man behind it, looking down at a tablet in his lap, asked, "What you need?"

She replied, "I've got some unique items from the other planet. I've been told I could get a good price for them here."

He set the tablet aside and raised an eyebrow. "Do you have proof of provenance?"

She shook her head. "This is a 'finders keepers' sort of thing."

"It'll decrease what I can give you for them."

"Of course. I fully understand. I'm thinking fifteen hundred for each." She placed the stones on the desk.

He made a show of pulling out a jeweler's loupe and looking at them carefully, then replied, "Best I can do is six hundred."

She stopped herself from rolling her eyes at the lowball offer. "Two thousand five hundred total."

"Seven-fifty each."

They negotiated good-naturedly to a final price of nineteen hundred dollars total, which was slightly less than she'd hoped for but adequate for her needs. Before she left, he said, "Anything else you wind up finding and keeping, bring it by. I'm happy to take a look."

She smiled. "Will do. Good to know you."

Another car took her to Abstention. She entered through the front door and slipped the man who greeted her inside a fifty-dollar bill as she asked, "Which dice table is the hottest?"

He nodded at a craps game in the corner, an oval surrounded by cheering and shouting people. "That one's blazing. It should stay that way for a little while."

She gave him a nod. "If that turns out to be true, I'll match that. Could you have someone send over a drink for me?"

"Of course." The place looked like it had an identity crisis. There was an attempt at elegance, like the tuxedoed maître d' she'd spoken to, but the clientele was largely not as well-dressed, consistent with those who'd entered the night before. Their attitudes and behaviors didn't speak of old money but of a more modern sensibility toward wealth. *Like, it's for spending on entertainment.*

She joined the table and laid bets for herself and the dealers, cheering on the other players. A drink arrived in short order, a martini with three green olives. She sipped it just enough to dampen her tongue, then pretended to forget about it as she got back into the game. By the time she was done, she'd played through several thousand dollars and was up five hundred.

She returned to the maître d' and slipped him the bill she'd promised. "Thanks. I'm interested in some fun tonight and looking for some Magic Flame." She surreptitiously held out yet another fifty. "Know somewhere I could find that?"

He nodded toward the rear. "Go through the videogame area. There's a door in the back. Tell them Charlie sent you."

She replied, "Thanks. Again, if it works out, double that for you."

He swallowed once, then amended, "Say Charles sent you instead."

"Will do."

Aza whispered, *Remember, just start screaming if you need*

help. She wondered if he was able to hear her conversation through the building or if he'd just lucked out with the timing.

When she reached the back after weaving her way through individuals wearing VR rigs, she offered the code-word as instructed and was admitted to a room that had the look of an elegant bar from the early nineteen hundreds, with an exclusively well-dressed clientele. It was all in blues and dim lighting, leather couches around the periphery filled with people drinking, talking, and making out. When the bartender noticed her, he came over and asked, "What are you looking for?"

She replied, "Magic Flame and," she lowered her voice, "access to a certain piece of specialized equipment."

He nodded at an empty corner of the room. "Stand over there."

She did so, knowing that a security system was scanning her. *Hopefully looking in the Boston PD's databases.* After a couple of minutes, a burly man in a tailored vintage suit walked up to her. "Okay, you're good. You can pick up the fire from the bartender on your way out." He pushed aside the curtain behind her and opened the door it revealed, which led to a staircase going down. "Enjoy."

CHAPTER EIGHTEEN

What awaited her at the bottom of the stairs was unlike what she'd imagined the Purple Market to be. She'd assumed it would be like a mall, or maybe a bazaar, with stands set up for proprietors to sell their wares. Instead, the atmosphere was more like a flea market, with tables arranged in rows and people seated behind them.

It wasn't quite a flea market, either since the folks at each of the tables weren't waiting to sell. Everyone was fiddling with things, building things, or working on things. She laughed inwardly. *It's like a crafting party!*. Arcade-style video games were positioned around the perimeter, either antiques or new machines designed to resemble antiques, with people laughing, placing bets, and competing on them. She stepped out of the pathway as a burly bearded man hustled by to greet someone who had come in behind her with a shriek of joy and a large hug.

She wandered around, gazing down at the tables she passed. No one looked up to meet her eye but kept doing their own thing. *Weird.* She surreptitiously watched the other people who looked like customers meandering among the tables. They were better dressed than those who were seated. When they wanted to talk, they would offer a polite "Excuse me," and wait for the person at the table to finish what they were doing and transfer their attention to them. For an illegal underground market—*at least for tax purposes, as I doubt these folks declare their sales*—it was remarkably genteel.

A voice came from her side, filled with good humor. "Must be your first time. You've got that look."

She turned to see a dark-skinned man in a fedora, his eyes large behind his thick glasses. He was wearing a garish bowling shirt and ironed jeans. "Yeah, you're right."

He nodded. "I love being right. Billy's my name. I serve as the welcome wagon here in our corner of the Purple Market."

"I was starting to wonder if that name was real or only a rumor."

"Oh, it's real, but the market is less a place than an ideal. This isn't the only one."

He patted the stool beside him and she sat on it, putting her back to the wall like he did. "Are they all coordinated?"

He replied, "Naw. Each does its own thing. By the way, this is where I must inquire if you're law enforcement."

Cait laughed. "Nothing to worry about there. I'm Lexi, and I'm in business for myself. Definitely not a cop."

He nodded genially. "Good to know. We have to ask every stranger, you understand. We've got a cool, calm, groovy thing going on here. This isn't the kind of place you go to find something that's gonna hurt someone, for instance. I wouldn't be part of that."

"Nothing wrong with providing a service to those who need it, under those conditions."

"Exactly." Cait had no issue with denying that she was a marshal in this setting since her purpose wasn't to build a case or arrest anyone. The deception didn't endanger anyone except maybe her. He said, "Now, I like to play a game where I figure out what people are searching for." He made a show of looking her up and down. "Maybe something that works on magical alarms?"

She laughed. "Come on. Your boy upstairs pulled my sheet and told you what he found."

Billy grinned, showing slightly crooked teeth in a smile. "Guilty as charged. Doesn't mean I'm wrong, does it?"

She leaned over so her voice wouldn't carry. "I'm looking for something that will allow me to get into places that people might not want me to be in. That's true. But not an alarm neutralizer."

He considered her, then suggested, "Lock picks?"

Cait grinned. "Nope. If you miss it three times, do I get a prize?"

He laughed again. "I like you. No, no prize, but I'll buy you a drink, win or lose." He gestured with his chin to a tub of ice filled with bottles of beer.

"Deal. What's your third guess?"

He made a show of thinking about it, then said, "Nope. I've got nothing. You tell me."

She grinned. "Make with the beer first." He waved, and someone brought over a couple of bottles and popped the tops. He offered her the opportunity to choose, and after she selected one, drank from his. She lifted the bottle in thanks for the effort to remove suspicion from the exchange and took a swig from hers. "I'm looking for a portal beacon."

He nodded. "Makes sense. I figured you'd be one to work alone, though, and if you're already there, you know where to portal to, right?"

"You can't always be sure you can handle a, uh, task alone. A girl's got to have options."

"Let me think about that." They drank in silence. Eventually, he nodded toward the far corner. "Jasper over there does some good work with transport-related things. He might be the right person to talk to."

She finished her drink and slid off the seat. "Thanks for your help, Billy. Anything I can do in return?"

He smiled. "We'll call it you owing me one. See what happens in the future."

"Fair enough. Good to meet you."

"Likewise."

She casually made her way through the space, careful not to appear as if she was headed directly for the man Billy had recommended. When she reached him, she waited for a pause in his work, then said, "Excuse me?"

He looked up at her and grunted. He had a long beard that initially came off as scruffy, but on closer appearance, it was well-maintained. His lips were hidden by the mustache that went with it. Jeans and a black t-shirt finished the look. "Saw you chatting with Billy. He send you over here?"

"Yeah."

He gestured to the side of the table. "Have a seat." She did, and he continued, "What can Jasper do for you?"

"Well, Jasper, I'm Lexi. I'm interested in being able to portal to somewhere I haven't been."

He nodded. "A beacon, then. That can be entirely magical, or part tech, part magic. Do you have a preference, one or the other?"

She shrugged. "Guess I don't know enough about it to say. What are the advantages?"

"Magical, harder to detect, but potentially drains before it can be used if anti-magic emitters or other unexpected circumstances are part of the picture. Technomagical, I put a sensor on there that keeps the magic part dormant until a given condition is met. It could be a motion detector, sound detector, whatever kind of equipment you want to stick on it."

"The latter seems more versatile."

He raised a palm in agreement. "The only additional risk is that its sensors are not completely passive. Normally, the signal is so low that it's impossible to detect until you're right on it."

Yeah, I've had experience with that. "Do you make those yourself?"

"I have someone who shares the work with me, but we're the main sources in Boston."

"Well, then, I'd love to arrange to get one from you."

He leaned back in his chair, staring into her eyes. "I'll have to check you out first. Standard operating procedure. You understand." He scribbled on a card and slid it over. "Visit this website after tomorrow. It'll give you a way to contact me if I decide I'm willing to work with you."

She nodded. "Will do."

"One word of warning. Any funny stuff, like trying to track me through there, gets you blacklisted by all of us at every market. We stick together."

Cait grinned. "Wouldn't have it any other way. Talk to you soon, Jasper."

CHAPTER NINETEEN

After finishing at the Purple Market, Cait returned to the hotel, hurriedly packed a bag, and portaled to her family's house. She arrived around eleven and was surprised when no one rushed out to meet her. Concerned, she entered the house warily, only to discover there was a very good reason her arrival had been ignored.

Sitting at the far end of the brunch table, across from her smiling mother, was her father Lewis. He rose at her appearance and she ran to give him a hug, which he returned enthusiastically. His strength always came as a surprise because, though he wasn't athletic, he didn't carry himself as someone with the kind of power he had. She said, "It's so good to see you. Finally decide you could deal with Mom again, huh?"

He laughed, and as they took their seats, her mother replied, "Hush." Moira reached over to pat the dragon, who had immediately sat beside her chair. "Lewis, this is Aza, the newest member of the family."

He replied, "Well, come over here and let me have a look at you."

The dragon complied, and her father looked first at one of his sides, then the other. "Camouflage scales, yes?" Aza rippled them. "Yeah, the rainbow hue is a dead giveaway. Gorgeous. I understand you're stuck with my daughter?"

Aza snorted. *Oh, I like him.*

Cait rolled her eyes. "He says your sense of humor is terrible, and you should stop talking." Aza gave a soft growl, and she sighed. "Fine. He likes you."

"So, he communicates telepathically?"

"He does. Do all dragons?"

Her father shook her head. "Some speak humanoid languages. It's a magical conversion, from what I've read. I'm not positive their mouths and throats are structured to make sounds that we would recognize as speech. They're quite good at roaring, though."

Brianna interrupted, "So, talking about Cait and the poor dragon who's doomed to be her companion is boring. Tell us what you've been up to, Dad."

Cait stuck her tongue out at her sister, and the other woman responded in kind. Moira scowled. "Children. Behave."

The smile on her father's face showed that *he* was amused by their banter. "Oh, a little of this and a bit of that, as usual. Lately, I've been visiting Drow ruins, learning what I can about how they used to live. I found some interesting things to add to each of your collections." He gestured at a bulging, much-abused leather backpack leaning against the wall next to a pair of stout walking sticks.

Aisling asked, "Why the particular interest in the dark elves?"

He shrugged. "I haven't spent a lot of time learning about them, and it seemed like the right moment. No specific reason."

Moira asked, "So, you'll be staying for a while?" Cait heard the note of hope in her mother's voice.

Her father offered her mother a soft smile. The love they felt for one another radiated across the table. "A few weeks, at least. Until the urge to wander grows too strong to ignore, as it always does."

Moira nodded and echoed, "As it always does."

He laughed. "You knew what I was like when you married me."

She grinned. "It's true, I did. No regrets. If you were here all the time, we'd probably wind up killing each other. What kind of example would that set for the coven?"

Brianna corrected, "Well, no regrets aside from Cait. That's a *huge* regret. But at least you got a pair of quality children with Aisling and me."

Cait said dryly, "Aza, burn her."

He snorted in her mind but didn't otherwise respond.

Brianna's eyebrows twitched upward. "Aw, he doesn't like you anymore?"

Cait's answer was both considerate and mature, she thought, as she hurled a biscuit across the table at her sister. Her parents shouted at her to stop in unison, and Cait grinned. *It's good to have all of us together again.*

After they'd finished their meal, they stayed at the table, sipping coffee and tea and munching on scones and jam. Moira said, "The wolves've been quiet, but I believe we need to repay them in kind. Tomorrow is the full moon, and I imagine they will have a gathering of some sort."

Her father replied, "And you plan to what? Just drop in?"

Her mother shrugged. "More or less."

Lewis shook his head. "If we're going to do it, we should do it as a family."

Cait, sensing they were on the threshold of a long and irritating conversation, interjected, "How are our defenses coming?"

Brianna answered, "We've set up a night watch. Four at a time, four-hour sessions, one patrolling in each direction. Everyone's taking a turn."

"So, we'll get a warning if they attack. That's a good start. What else?"

Aisling replied, "I've almost got an alarm web ready to go. I've been putting devices in place as fast as I can acquire or build them. They're not complicated, just a power source, a wireless card, and magic and motion detectors. That way, if the shifters try to come in, even under illusion, we'll catch them at it."

Cait asked, "Can shifters use magic other than their innate variety?"

No one answered, and her father shrugged. "One of many unknowns about shifters. They could always hire assistance, so it's a good plan, regardless."

Brianna replied, "Everyone is ready to fight to defend our homes."

"Speaking of which," Cait replied, "I should do something about getting another wand like Sashura told me to."

Her father nodded. "Your mother told me you needed one shortly after you found out."

"Do you know where to find one?"

"I've been looking. I think I know where your grandmother got hers, but it's not safe to go there."

Cait chuckled. "Seems like nothing is safe these days. That's fine. I can deal with it."

Aisling replied, "I'm coming too." Everyone except Aza replied with some form of negation. Aisling shook her head. "Historic magical sites are my thing. I studied them for ages as part of learning technomancy. If you're visiting one, I need to be there. Like I said, I'm coming along."

Her father shrugged. "Well, when you put it like that, guess I can't argue. We might as well do it now so we can be back in time for the full moon. Go get yourselves ready."

Cait and Aisling raced for the stairs, her younger sister reaching them a step before she did. Cait growled, "Home field advantage. You're still slow."

Her sister laughed. "It's your home field too, or it would be if you spent more time here."

"Stop. You're channeling Mother."

Her sister waved and darted into her room, slamming the door behind her in her haste. Cait entered her own and pulled off her traveling clothes, replacing them with the thick leather outfit she wore when danger threatened. Her daggers, in their wrist sheaths, went on next, her bracelet expanding onto her forearm to accommodate them.

She grabbed a backpack and checked her survival supplies, then put on her best hiking boots and hefted her shillelagh. Aza watched her preparations and provided a running commentary of his opinion on her choices throughout. She told him, "Sometimes I think Aisling is right. A stick seems less useful than a sword."

The dragon replied, "I'm guessing the skills would transfer pretty easily if you decided to switch."

"But there's something about this." She twirled it. "Maybe it's just how often I've gotten to hit Brianna with it. So many happy memories."

He laughed. "Perhaps you should fight with one sword and one stick?"

She shook her head. "Then I wouldn't be able to cast. I need to keep one hand free for magic."

He stretched and replied, "Makes sense."

Cait sighed. "I'm procrastinating, aren't I?"

"Definitely. Nervous?"

"Maybe. Being around my dad is always great, but also always kind of weird since he's absent so much."

"It's good to be aware of what makes you happy in life and embrace that like he has. You could maybe take a lesson if you ever quit running from problem to problem long enough to figure out what it is that sparks your joy."

She sighed. "No one likes you."

"Your family does. More than they like you, I think."

"Great. Another traitor in my life." She shook her head with a smile. "Let's go to Oriceran, fang face."

CHAPTER TWENTY

Cait and Aza arrived downstairs before her sister and waited quietly, not wanting to interrupt her father's conversation with her mother. Sounds of cleaning came from the kitchen as Brianna gave their parents what privacy she could.

Seeing the two of them together always made Cait smile. She didn't understand how two people who loved each other so deeply could be so accepting of how much time they spent apart. But, since her expertise in successful relationships was lacking, she figured it wasn't her place to judge. She'd had a few boyfriends, but no one who had inspired her to look at him the way her parents looked at each other.

Aza asked, *Is that what love looks like for humans?*

Cait whispered, "Yeah. I think so."

He gave his version of a frown. *Seems mushy.*

She muffled her laughter with a hand. "That, my friend, is a fair assessment. Do dragons fall in love?"

He fluttered his wings. *I don't know. I guess I'll figure that out when I'm older.*

"Suddenly, I have the vision of you acting like a human teenager. All obsessed with dating, getting your heart broken, and flouncing around in great emotional distress."

I would never flounce.

The laughter escaped her. "You'd be like, 'Oh, my heart is breaking.' Flounce. Flop."

He growled. *I will bite you. Don't think I won't.*

"Oh, the pain! Oh, the great, immense, heartrending *anguish*!"

He bumped into her leg hard enough to knock her aside despite only being the size of a medium dog.

She laughed some more, then wiped her eyes and sighed. "I'm sorry. I'm done. Thank you though. I really needed that."

Aisling, bounding down the stairs, asked, "Needed what?"

Cait shook her head. "Aza's being funny, that's all."

Her sister wrapped the dragon in a hug. "You're too good for her. You should come with me instead."

Cait replied instantly, "He says he can't think of a worse fate."

Aza countered, *I did not.* Cait remained quiet, and a moment later, her companion continued, *I'm not able to speak with her telepathically. You tell her the truth, or I'll bite you. Right now.*

She laughed. "Fine. He didn't say that. I did."

Aisling, who was still hugging the dragon, replied, "Oh, I figured. He's much smarter and nicer than you. Better-looking too."

Her father's hand fell on her shoulder, and she swiveled her head to see him smiling. "Let's get going, kids. We're on a timetable."

After they'd said their goodbyes, they headed for the backyard, where her father had opened a portal to Oriceran. They stepped through, and he let it fall closed behind them. Cait stared around since visits to the other planet were still novel despite the times she'd been there with her father on one expedition or another. He seemed different on the magic world, as if a subtle tension he'd held at home, separate from his obvious happiness, had evaporated. He was dressed in his exploration clothes of heavy denim jeans, a couple of layers of shirts, serious hiking boots, and a leather jacket. Aisling wore an almost identical outfit and had her paired swords on her back.

Her father said, "I've read your grandmother's journals and tried to find out where she got her wand. Unfortunately, she wasn't exactly a scientist in terms of describing her experiences. It's all very indirect. No map, just references to locations that may or may not still exist. Nonetheless, I believe I've figured out where the place is. It's about an hour's walk from here. If the trees weren't so thick, we'd be able to see it since it's on top of a small mountain."

Cait asked, "Does it need to be from the same spot? Wouldn't any tree from Oriceran do?"

He shook his head. "Magic flows and is subtly different in different places. While any wand might work, one from the same location as where your magic is originally from would function best. That's for a single wand. Where double wands are concerned, ideally, you want them from the same tree so they'll have the greatest affinity between them."

Aisling asked, "What does that do?"

"Makes the effort of using them together far easier. Mentally, they operate with far less resistance than if you're trying to join unrelated things. At least, that's what everything I've read says." That was as much of an answer as he was willing to give, and he urged them into motion. As they walked, he said, "To be fair, the journal isn't all that bad. It's simply written from her limited perspective rather than from a wider view. I guess that's one of the benefits you get as you age. She was young when she went for her wand, barely a teenager. Another problem is that the land has changed in the years since she was here."

He continued to talk about Oriceran and the places he'd been as they walked. Cait loved listening to his stories and thought maybe that was one of the things that made it easier for her mother to bear their separations, the fact that he was so visibly happy when he shared the tales afterward.

They emerged from the forest, and he gestured up at a mountain in the near distance. It was rocky and sheer, and the top was occluded by a mist that seemed to start halfway up and surrounded it all the way into the sky. "Once, in your grandmother's time, a path apparently led up the side of the mountain. But something happened, and now it's just steep rock, from the looks of it."

Lewis shook his head. "Naturally, the tree is on the top.

So, to reach it, our best bet is probably to go through the inside path she mentions. She didn't take it, so she didn't describe it. Only said one existed and that she walked a little way in before deciding that she preferred to climb in the sun."

Aza offered, *I could fly up there and take a look around.*

Her father nodded after she related the dragon's words. "Excellent idea. Go ahead and try."

They watched as he flew toward the mountain. When he reached the mist, lightning crashed and forced him to veer away. He circled and tried again from a different angle, but more lightning blocked his path. He growled angry words in her mind as he tried several more times, then flew back, defeated. *I can't get there.*

Aisling asked, "What's going on?"

Her father shook his head. "Something bad. Something evil, perhaps."

Cait suggested, "Related to the wand?"

"No way to say."

"This is the only option?"

He shrugged. "It's the best option for your magic, and perhaps we are meant to be here."

Cait chuckled. "Bad karma?"

Lewis offered a thin smile. "Or Fate. Your grandmother was drawn to this place. Now, two generations later, you are too. That could be a coincidence. It could also have significance."

Aisling said, "No way to tell without going inside," and marched ahead. They followed, reaching the mountain thirty minutes later. They paused to eat the scones they'd brought along and drink from their canteens before continuing. Her father waved his hand, activating the wand bracelet he wore, and the entrance to the cave described in the journal was illuminated. The light flowed out of him as they walked inside. Her sister observed, "This is all worked stone. With tools, it looks like, rather than magic. I can't tell if those are stacked blocks or if they're carved out of the wall to resemble them."

Her father replied, "Carved, I think. Not functional, just ornamental."

Cait didn't have an opinion. Aza said, *I think I'm not a fan of caves.*

She laughed, thinking back to the battles she'd fought in the mountain on the way to meeting her partner. "Right?"

Her father asked, "What?"

Cait shook her head. "Just answering Aza." They stopped when they came to a circular ramp. To the right, it spiraled upward, and to the left, downward. It was as if someone had stuck a drill in the top of the mountain and pushed it inside, carving out the path and a central cylinder. "So, the wand's at the top, yeah?"

Her father confirmed that, and Aisling said, "I feel like we need to investigate what's below, though."

Lewis nodded. "I agree."

Cait realized she also wanted to know what was down there and sighed. "All right, we'll do it. Carefully. If something kills us here, Mom's going to be really ticked at you, Dad."

He laughed. "Wouldn't want that. Her wrath is fierce and frightening. Let's make sure that doesn't happen."

CHAPTER TWENTY-ONE

Her father led the way down, the light blazing out in front of him. Her sister was second, and she and Aza walked side by side despite the narrowness of the descent. After a few moments, Aza shrank to his tiny size and leapt onto her shoulder, his talons digging into the leather for balance. Partway down, their father stopped. Aisling said, "I was about to warn you."

He nodded. "Good. It's not very sophisticated, but I'm not sure what it will do. Let's back up a little." They did so, and her father gestured forward, creating a shimmering block of force in the air. He asked, "Ready?"

Aisling replied, "Yep." Cait echoed her.

He dropped the block. It landed on a pressure plate they'd both apparently spotted. *I would've seen it too if they hadn't blocked my view.* Her inner voice laughed. *Sure you would have. Shut up, you. Me. Whatever.*

Spikes shot out of the wall through disguised holes at head and knee level. They retracted after a moment.

Aisling whistled. "They apparently don't believe in warnings."

Cait replied, "Perhaps they considered scary tunnels under an obviously evil mountain to be sufficient dissuasion?"

Her father chuckled darkly. "No way to tell, but I will say one thing. I'm glad your grandmother didn't come in here. Might have snipped off the family tree right there if she had."

With that somber thought, they continued circling down. They found several more traps along the path, all pressure plates. They passed by triggering them, then covering them with a box of force magic as they crossed over. At one point, two were positioned in a row, presumably in the hope that the second would catch someone who avoided the first. Aza whispered, *It's a good thing your family has experience with this stuff.*

"It is." She didn't say more, not wanting to distract her father and sister from their search for hidden dangers. Finally, they reached the bottom of the spiral. It ended at a large set of double doors made of carved stone that was different from the surrounding walls. The large slabs could not have been brought down the staircase, so she assumed magic had been involved. The doors were decorated with glyphs she couldn't make heads or tails of, but the number of locks securing the doors caught her eye. "I'm not the only one noticing that those locks are on the outside, right? As if they're trying to hold something in?"

Her father replied, "That had occurred to me."

Aisling said, "Maybe it is a bad idea to go in there." Her voice held more excitement than fear, though.

Lewis said, "Does anyone want to go up and find the wand without discovering what's back there?" Even Cait didn't reply. He withdrew his second walking stick from where it hung on his backpack so that he held one in each hand. Aisling drew her swords. Cait gripped her shillelagh tighter. "Okay, then. Let's open it up."

They undid the locks one by one, careful to check each for traps before interacting with it. A gesture from her father pulled the doors open, and they stepped inside. The chamber was far larger than Cait would've expected, given the narrowness of the path to reach it. As they crossed the threshold, torches in wall sconces erupted in flames.

They froze as the illumination grew. It revealed the sort of things Cait had seen on documentaries about the tombs of Egypt. Two sarcophagi sat on the floor, the carved faces on the top looking at the ceiling or perhaps toward heaven. Long-fingered hands held scepters. The one on the left was clearly male; the one on the right, slightly smaller in stature, was presumably female, although time had blurred the features enough that she wouldn't bet her life on it. Her inner voice snarked, *Great word choice, given where you are at the moment.*

Shut. Up. Stacked around the room were treasure chests and urns, along with items of pottery, stone figures, and other less identifiable objects. Aisling said, "Looks vaguely Egyptian."

Her father concurred. "I was thinking that, too."

"Things like this make me wonder if the gates connecting the planets were open far earlier than most people think."

"I've wondered the same at any number of locations.

They *had* to be, unless we're buying into the theory that some alien race seeded both planets."

Cait replied, "That's just as likely if you ask me."

Aisling laughed. "No one was. Now, take your uneducated brain and put it to use looking around. Try not to touch anything, though."

Cait scowled. "I'm not an idiot."

Aza snorted in her mind. "Your family seems to think you are."

She moved carefully through the space, thinking about all the movies she'd seen that started off with a scenario like this and ended with someone getting a terrible curse. A sudden grinding sound caused her to look down at her hands to make sure she hadn't touched anything, then at her feet to see if she'd stepped on a pressure plate. Finally, she looked at the ceiling scraping down toward them. Her father observed, "Slow crushing death. Lovely." His tone hadn't changed, and it communicated interest, not fear.

Aisling sounded more alarmed, but not much. "We can lie on the floor between the sarcophagi and on either side of them. They're not going to crush their rulers or whoever's inside there."

Lewis agreed, and they moved into position. It offered safety...until the spikes emerged from the ceiling, each longer than the sarcophagi were tall. Cait said, "I think a more active defense might be necessary."

Her father called, "Shields first, then push it back up."

She complied, and her sister did the same. As their magic hit it, the ceiling stopped descending and started to move back up. When it passed the level it had been at before, a click echoed through the chamber. Her father ordered, "Okay, let it drop slowly." It dropped a couple of inches and locked into place.

Cait said, "I don't think we should trust it. Let's throw up some pillars."

The others agreed, and they placed supports around the room. Then they opened the sarcophagi, figuring they'd already identified the room's deadliest danger. They did so fully shielded, so when they triggered a dart trap, it failed to damage them. She scowled at the revelation that the first sarcophagus was empty, and her frown grew deeper upon discovering the second was as well. Aisling said, "Guess we could've hidden in there from the drop ceiling."

She shook her head with a laugh at the dumb joke. "Lovely. And you two enjoy this, do you?"

Her father laughed. "Of course." He reached into the sarcophagus and did something, and a part of the rear wall sank backward, then slid aside. They entered the chamber beyond and found two larger-than-life-sized figures seated on carved stone thrones.

The strange constructions were made of golden metal, joints articulated with visible gears, skulls glowing in the torchlight. They looked like oversized skeletons that an ambitious metalworker had gilded. Cait shouted in alarmed surprise when they moved and instinctively side-stepped toward the left as Aisling and her father moved right.

Aza hopped down from her shoulder and grew to Great Dane size, then stood alertly at her side. The golden pair stood and looked around the room robotically in an eerie imitation of life. Aisling said, "Technomancy for sure. Probably a power source inside the head. It doesn't have anything replacing muscles, so the motion must be magical, too. The gears are definitely technology. Weird. I've never seen it's like before."

A shudder ran through the figures, and blades extended from their palms. They were as long as the forearms. Cait observed, "That's not good." She brought her shillelagh up and cast a second force shield around herself. She would have liked to do the same for Aza, but he preferred to have access to all his skills rather than being unable to breathe fire because he was within a magical orb. Cait couldn't argue, even though she wanted to.

In a blur of unexpectedly smooth motion, the magical automatons attacked.

CHAPTER TWENTY-TWO

The magical robots, which was the best way to categorize them as near as Cait could tell, split up, one moving to attack Aisling and her father, the other headed toward her and Aza. She snapped, "Keep an eye on them. If you think they need help, go."

Aza replied, "Yes." They spread apart as the automaton made its first swing, whipping both of its arms in perfect horizontal strikes from outside in, then from inside to out. She dodged easily, and the blades never came close to Aza, who simply ducked to avoid them.

She growled, "These things are bizarre, but if their attacks remain simple, we should have no problem taking them down." Unfortunately, the next strikes were wickedly fast diagonals, the blades hissing as they cut through the air. The ones after that were curves, and she had to interpose her shillelagh to block the swords since they were too quick to deal with one at a time.

The robot began to operate the blades separately. Cait backpedaled from the whirling weapons, which were now moving too fast for her to defend against. She pushed power into her muscles, increasing her own speed, and tried to take her brain out of her immediate defense to allow her body to work without the delay of thinking.

Aza darted in from the side and whipped his tail around, slamming it into the back of the thing's knees. The attack would have dropped a human of any size, she imagined. It failed to move the giant metal skeleton. The blade attacks continued unabated as the robot kicked at the dragon, narrowly missing him as he scrambled out of the way. She called, "These things are a bit harder than I thought. Any suggestions from the brainy people?"

Aisling didn't have time to laugh at her sister's question. The behemoth attacking her and her father had sped up substantially since first engaging them, and they were now faced with a blur of sharp metal. When those attacks came toward her, her swords deftly picked off the incoming weapons, but her counters, when she managed any, didn't come close to connecting. She shouted, "We need to slow them down," and to her father, "Cover me."

He lifted both his sticks, which were enchanted and able to withstand the impact of their enemy's blades. She dodged behind him, and his weapons flew out to intercept the incoming attacks, knocking them aside with impressive speed. They bounced out wider than when she blocked, reminding her of her father's remarkable strength.

The floor was covered with dirt mixed with sand that

had accumulated over time. She reached for her magic and used force to create an air current, waving her hand to build a small tornado that lifted the particles from the ground and concentrated them into a smaller space, pressing them together.

She waited for an opportunity to present itself. When the automaton took a step, bending its legs at the knees to do so, she blasted the dirt and sand directly into the joint, hoping to muck up the gears. She repeated the process with the other leg when it moved next, then returned to the fight, stepping up beside her father and instructing, "Let's get it moving."

Aisling circled to the right, and her father followed close on her heels. The automaton obediently pursued them both, leading with its whirling blades. *All right, bastard, here's hoping you're mechanical enough that messing up your gears works.*

Cait watched her father and sister out of the corner of her eye as she fought her enemy. Aza had bathed it in a gout of fire, which seemed to alarm it, judging by the speed with which it moved out of the way. *Mobility is the big issue. It attacks too fast, and it moves too fast. Maybe Aisling has the right idea. Let's slow it down.* She called, "Aza, keep it in place for a minute."

The dragon leapt into the air and flew at the golden skeleton, which shifted into defensive mode to address the new assault. She extended her arm, pointed a finger, and dispatched a jet of ice and frost, focusing it on one knee joint. The area frosted over, then ice hardened around it. Aza flew away, and it tried to follow him. The ice cracked and broke, and it stumbled. *Gotcha, metal head.* She shouted, "Keep it moving. I'll freeze it, and when it moves afterward, we'll attack."

Aza replied, *Good plan.* His voice held excitement but no fear or worry.

You're something, buddy, Cait told him.

She defended against several more blows, then locked its knee with ice again. When it moved and stumbled, she brought her shillelagh around in a powerful strike, aided by the magic she'd added to her muscles. The weapon slammed into its upper arm, denting the metal. It paused, manipulated the arm as if verifying it still worked, then stomped toward her behind a series of wicked slashes. Even though its face was immobile and the skull lacked eyes to convey emotion, she got the impression she'd angered it. "Uh-oh. I don't think it liked that."

Aza replied, *I get the same feeling.*

Aisling had seen her sister steal her strategy, using direct magic instead of dirt. When she noticed their robot slowing down as its joints abraded and locked up, she knew what she had to do. She circled behind her father again and summoned a larger vortex, gathering more dust and dirt and giving it a few seconds to compress.

When the funnel was fully laden, she moved it across the floor until it covered the automaton and held it there, bathing the robot in grit. She was forced to release the magic ten seconds later when her foe extended a palm and launched the blade that extended from that hand at her.

Aisling yelped and fell backward, the unexpected projectile scraping off her force shield as she dropped. Her father called, "Watch out for flying swords." Cait cursed in acknowledgment. Aisling forced herself to her feet and drew her weapons again, ready to go after it now that it had weakened itself. She took a step toward the unbladed side of the robot, but another sword emerged from its palm. She growled, "Dammit, it's got reloads. Not cool."

What *was* cool was that the metal skeleton was moving with a stutter, and an audible grinding sound was emanating from its joints. She laughed. "I think we've got it."

Her father replied, "You take left. I'll take right. We'll meet in the middle."

With a nod and a grin, she waded in. With a foe on either side, it engaged them both, although logistics limited it to one blade against each. She blocked its strike with a sword, then chopped down at its elbow with the other. Her weapon didn't penetrate, but it did put a crease in the metal. "This might take a while."

A loud clang sounded as her father smashed his shillelagh into the thing's head. It turned to face him and twisted a little in his direction. She slashed at its leg, drawing its attention back to her, but she would have bet money that its blades were now moving even faster. "I think you made it mad."

The killing blow landed mostly by luck. Cait had frozen it, having shifted to a less structured approach of throwing ice at it. It had built up around the robot's neck, and when Aza flew in and blasted it with fire, the supercooled metal shattered.

Its head toppled off, bouncing off an arm on the way to the floor, and the body went still. She turned, ready to help Aisling and her father, but they didn't need assistance. Their opponent was moving in stutters and jerks, and they took turns slamming it in the head with their weapons. A minute later, a forehand swing by her father knocked its head free, taking the monstrosity out of the fight.

It stood immobile until Aisling jump-kicked it, knocking it to the ground. She stalked over to the skull and picked it up, then regarded it carefully, holding it up to the light. She whispered and waved her wand bracelet. "Yep, power crystal inside. Not sure I can get it out without better tools, so let's take the heads with us."

Cait laughed, then whined, "But they're heavy."

Their father responded with a snort. "I'll carry them. Goofballs. I wonder how this is connected to the mist at the top of the mountain?"

Aisling replied, "Maybe it was a signal? An automated process that activated at a certain time?"

"Possible. Or maybe the seismic event that took out the path set it off. Maybe," he said, his voice thoughtful, "it was some religion or community that believed it could be brought back in the future, and the mist was a signal to reassemble."

Cait shrugged. "All I know is that the undead versions

of themselves they left behind sucked royally—heh, get it? *Royally*—and we need to go get my wand."

Her father paced around the chamber before they departed, gathering up the heads and several other objects he said looked valuable. As they climbed the spiral stairs, he ventured, "The designs down there and on the objects look vaguely Elven, but not of any variety I recognize. They might've originated from the same root language, though."

Aisling replied, "I can't see anyone but the Drow doing something like this."

He shrugged. "There may have been other kinds of elves we know nothing about. It doesn't quite match the Drow language, and I haven't seen anything resembling this in any of their ruins or the books I've read about them."

Finally, they reached the summit. When they climbed the final steps onto it, they found only a single tree, green and healthy, present on the top. They could also see the countryside for miles in every direction. The mist had dissipated while they were inside. Aisling and her father fell into a discussion of why that might have happened as she approached the tree.

Cait put her right hand on the trunk and felt an immediate connection between the tree and the wand on her wrist. *Guess Dad was correct.* Aza asked, *What was that?*

"You felt it?"

His head dipped in a nod. "Yes. A surge of rightness?" He seemed as unclear about how to describe what he'd felt as she was.

"Well-put. Yeah, the tree seems to recognize my wand."

Or me. She ran her hand up the trunk, then along the branches she could reach, waiting for a sign. When she set her hand on the third branch, the feeling of rightness grew. As she moved it to one of the smaller branches that jutted from it, she knew it was the correct one.

Cait whispered an apology, drew her right-hand dagger, since it seemed appropriate to use Oriceran metal for the purpose, and used it to cut the branch off the tree. As soon as it detached, sap flowed out of the damaged section, covered it, and hardened into a nub that looked identical to the rest of the bark.

She turned to the others. "I've got it. Let's go home."

CHAPTER TWENTY-THREE

When they portaled back to Earth, it was early enough on Sunday morning that Cait was able to go to Croagh Patrick to meditate. She took her new wand with her. The idea of leaving it behind bothered her, as if it were an essential part of her. She used it to clean up the rings and cast the warding spells. A swell of happy fondness flowed through her at the discovery that it was as natural to use as her former one had been. *Thanks, Grandma. Wherever you are, I owe you.*

The hardest part of the process was getting Aza to settle down and quit jabbering at her. He had found the fight against the automatons thrilling and wanted to dissect strategy. He was looking forward to their next combat adventure. She'd had to tell him to hush, which sounded alarmingly like her mother. Eventually, he'd settled down enough that she could slip into the appropriate mental state.

When she opened her eyes nine nines later, he was

staring into her face from inches away. She leaned back reflexively. "Whoa, not cool. Creepy, actually."

He laughed. "About time you're awake. So, what would be the best way to defend against those projectile blades? I was thinking you could wrap an enemy in a force shield, but would that protect them from your other attacks?" It was like the conversation before her meditation had just been on pause while she was mentally away.

With a sigh, she gathered up her things and portaled back to the village instead of walking, hopeful that others would be awake for him to expend his enthusiasm on. Fortunately, Brianna had woken up early, and Cait scraped the dragon onto her before heading upstairs to shower and dress.

When they all assembled for breakfast, the first order of business was for her father to tell the tale of their adventure. He related it with drama and humor in the right places, and everyone listened appreciatively, even Cait, who had been there. Aza threw in clarifications, some of which she shared with the others and some of which she didn't relate. Finally, when the storytelling was complete, her mother came back around to the overarching topic of the day. "So, this evening, we'll return the compliment the wolves paid us by visiting our gathering. It promises to be a cloudless night for the full moon. Circumstances couldn't be better to stop by and offer our salutations."

The expected argument materialized as everyone gave their opinion over which members of the family should go. Finally, Cait said, "It can't be all of us. If something goes wrong, there must still be three to lead the coven." The others fell silent at that comment as if the potential that they might not return from engaging the wolves hadn't occurred to them.

Brianna said, "Then I'll do it."

Cait replied, "You can't. You're a vital part of the community. And Mother can't, either, since she's the head of the family." She sent an apologetic look her father's way. "Sorry, Dad."

He laughed. "You don't marry a witch and then live with her coven without knowing your place in the hierarchy, Caitriona. No need to be concerned about my feelings on that topic."

"And it doesn't make sense for it to be Aisling, either."

Her sister bristled. "Why not? If you say it's because I'm the youngest, I'll smack you silly."

Her mother replied, "Because your technomancy skills are going to be incredibly valuable to the coven. Assuming you finish your final project and earn your degree."

Aisling rolled her eyes. "It'll get done. Honestly."

Cait shrugged. "So that leaves me."

Her father offered, "I can come along as backup."

She shook her head. "As much as I wish I could accept, I don't think that's wise. Whether they'll respect you as a member of the coven is an unknown. Whether they will try to kill you to weaken the family is another. I know you are more than able to take care of yourself, but I worry that a male presence gives them a plausible reason to attack. They're territorial, and sometimes that can extend to gender in humans."

Her mother added, "And magicals."

Cait nodded. "Right. So, the possibility that it might

happen here can't be ignored. Besides, I've got backup. Isn't that so, Aza?"

The dragon roared his agreement.

"All right then. I need to spend the day getting ready. You can go work the coven. Make sure everyone's okay. Have Dad tell his stories."

Her mother smiled, and in it was an understanding that Cait was babbling because she was anxious, as she had when she was a child. "You don't need to tell us how to handle the coven, Cait. You do your thing; we'll do ours."

She retreated upstairs to her room and pulled a basket out of her wardrobe. Sitting on the floor with it, she methodically took each piece of the fighting outfit she'd worn to Oriceran into her lap, wiped it clean, and treated it with oil. Where it was damaged, she used a plant-based adhesive the witches concocted to seal up tears and rents.

It took several hours for her to work through all of it. Then she retrieved a different concoction from the basket, one specially formulated to treat wood, and polished her shillelagh. Each coat of the paste-like goo added another layer of hardness as it seeped into the wood and bonded with the layers that had gone before. Where the striking surface became chipped or cracked from use, the paste filled in the gaps and reinforced the whole. She'd heard it described in terms similar to what happened to bone when it fused with other bone. Except, in this case, the result was always stronger than it had been before the procedure.

When darkness fell, she donned the clothes and headed downstairs to say goodbye to her family. Her mother handed over a metal flask, and when Cait popped it open, she found that it was filled with red liquid. She asked, "Is this what I think it is?"

Moira nodded. "It's from the first batch I've been able to create. We won't have to buy or trade for it anymore if it works as it should. I've tried it on small injuries, and it seems quite effective."

Cait grinned. "I'll take thirty for a start."

Her mother laughed. "Just making one container's worth takes hours and a cauldron full of material. Unless your wounds are life-threatening, you can probably get away with sips rather than gulps. Of course, if you have a doubt, drink it all. Your life is worth any amount of time I will spend replacing it."

She gave her mother a hug. "Thank you." In truth, the discovery would be a boon for the whole community. Cait had gotten out of the habit of carrying potions in Columbus because the job hadn't been that dangerous there. *Although, given the adventures in Boston so far, I should probably keep this with me from now on.* Her gear at the SOG had one healing and one energy potion since their missions always had the potential for extreme danger.

She headed outside into the darkness with Aza at her side. Wolves howling in the distance gave them their first vector, and after they left the thickest tree cover, Aza flew up above the canopy. He guided her toward the source of the sounds and confirmed he'd spotted a mixture of humanoid figures and wolves gathered.

When she emerged from the tree line into the rocky clearing, which was filled with uneven terrain and a smattering of boulders, she quipped, "For people who are so interested in forests, you sure did pick an uncomfortable meeting space for your nightly karaoke session. Shouldn't you all be running around hunting deer or something?"

Her appearance was greeted by growls from every direction, from both the wolves in wolf form and the ones in humanoid form. The man who had visited the coven's gathering, presumably the leader, stepped forward toward her, his features visible in the bright moonlight. His face was calm, and he wore the same leather pants he had worn before. Again, his feet were bare, and this time his chest was, too. He replied, "Greetings, witch. Have you come to tell us that you all are leaving as we asked?"

Cait laughed. "Hardly. As we told you before, it's not the Middle Ages, and that won't be happening."

He shrugged. "Unfortunate, and you will pay the price for your poor decision-making soon enough. But if not that, then why are you here?"

She imitated his shrug of a moment before. "Just came out to meet the neighbors, give you the once over, that sort of thing." She made a point of looking around the clearing, examining what she saw. "Pretty mangy bunch if you ask me. No offense."

He laughed, then threw his head back and howled. The sound was matched by those around her. Aza, flying above, said, *Just attack if that's what you're going to do. I'll be there in an instant. Fur burns really well.*

She winced at the vision that leapt into her mind. "I'm sorry, I don't speak wolf, so I'm not sure what you were trying to say. I came to see if we could find a middle ground where we exist in harmony, or each live apart without bothering the other."

"We cannot."

"You realize this will lead to blood and death."

He nodded. "More on your side than ours. That is acceptable to reclaim our territory."

She shook her head. "I think you'll discover we're not as weak as you seem to believe."

He bared his teeth in a grin. "Why don't we find out? In truth, given your trespass into our grove, we are within our rights to kill you. Instead, as a gesture toward the hope that you will leave our land in peace, we offer you combat with honor."

Adrenaline spiked inside her. Some part of her had guessed the night would end up with something like this occurring, and she'd thought herself resigned to it. Now she realized she was *eager* for it. *Maybe Brianna is rubbing off on me, and not in a good way.* "First blood?"

He inclined his head in a slight nod. "Acceptable for the moment. We'll call that another middle ground since you are not yet acquainted with our ways."

Cait knew that for all his words, he just wanted to get a sense of his enemy. That was fine. She shared that desire. "Very well. Let's do it."

CHAPTER TWENTY-FOUR

One of the humanoid wolves approached her, and the others moved to the sides, creating a circle for them to battle in. The man opposite her wore leather as well, shorts with a ragged edge that ended above his knees. His wide face sported a mustache and a scruffy beard that looked like it had last been trimmed by claws without a mirror.

His eyes reflected the moonlight, glowing silver in freaky otherworldliness. Cait patted the underside of her forearm, reassuring herself that her new wand was where she'd secured it. She tossed her shillelagh from left hand to right hand as they circled one another, giving it a twirl now and again. Her opponent was appropriately cautious, seemingly waiting for her to make the first move. He taunted, "Are you just going to walk around all night, witchling?" His voice was low and harsh like he had to force the words up out of his throat.

She replied, "You're supposedly the apex predator, so I

thought you'd lead this dance. If you don't have the stones for it, I'll be happy to."

"When you're on the ground bleeding, you'll wish you hadn't said that."

"I just wish you'd shut up and get on with it. Seriously, if this is all you bring to the table, I'm going to tell my people not to worry."

He snarled and darted at her, which was the response she'd anticipated. He whipped his right hand toward her in what she expected to be a punch. The attack turned out to be a slash with newly transformed paws instead of hands, the fingers ending in large, curved claws.

Cait leaned back and let the blow pass in front of her. Her reflex was to summon a force shield, but she felt as if the battle would be more impactful if she wasn't seen to be using magic. She whipped her shillelagh around in a tight circle, batting his hand aside, then poked the narrow end into his ribs as she circled out of the way.

He turned and snarled as if enraged. But now that she got a better look at his eyes, which were no longer reflecting the moon, she saw cunning in them and knew he was playing with her, feeling her out. She shuffled forward and made a looping swing with the shillelagh at about three-quarters of her top speed, just to see what he would do.

He stepped in and lashed out at her arm with his claws, but her evasion and the heavy leather kept them from penetrating. The glancing impact sent a shock through the limb, though. *Damn, he's strong.* Her primary attention was focused on his other hand, which jabbed at her stomach, curled into a fist.

Cait blocked down with her free hand, deflecting his punch to glance off her thigh as she twisted her hips. She snapped up a back fist into his face. He jerked his head away and took it on the cheek, and it drew no blood. They disengaged and again circled one another warily. He taunted, "You fight like a human."

She replied, "You have the brain of an animal, and not a particularly evolved one at that. I've got the better deal."

Growls sounded from around her, and she filed the animal comment away as a future tactic to irritate them. Her inner voice laughed. *As if you need special ways to irritate people.*

If you're going to speak, make yourself useful.

No further observations from subconscious Cait were forthcoming.

Aza, on the other hand, took the break in the action to say, *He's not fighting at full speed, and the others have created a circle around the outside. You won't be able to get out of there without having to fight for it.*

Cait nodded. *I know.* Hopefully, her partner saw the gesture. The wolf attacked again, recapturing her attention. He ran at her and leapt, changing in midair from human to wolf, his body morphing and twisting in a matter of seconds. The transformation was distracting, and it was a second before she threw herself to the side in a shoulder roll, barely avoiding his raking rear claws as he went by.

She rolled up immediately and had to bring her shillelagh around to block his snapping teeth since he'd pressed the attack. The blow didn't connect, but it did drive him away. He used his greater speed to try to get behind her, and she twisted to meet his next attack with another strike of her stick. Again, he avoided it.

Cait felt like the change in form put him at a disadvantage, which was an interesting fact she filed away for later use. When he leapt in at her once more, she whipped her club down in a block at his head, which was aimed at her midsection. But he transformed before he arrived, slamming into her in his human form and driving her backward, whipping his forehead down at her face.

She managed to duck and catch it bone-on-bone rather than letting him break her nose. She staggered back from the blow, dazed, and waved her shillelagh in front of her in a desperate block. Fortunately, he had also reeled back from the impact. As they circled, he no longer looked confident or condescending. He seemed angry, primal, and fiercely animalistic.

Cait felt similar emotions. The fight was engaging her complete attention in a way she couldn't recall experiencing before. Thus far, she'd kept it a physical battle, figuring that would have the greatest impact on the wolves. Aza suggested, "You should make yourself faster and stronger."

She had to agree. The battle had shifted, and she had little doubt that if he could draw blood and injure her severely at the same time, he would do so. Using an old familiar spell she no longer needed to speak, she infused power into her body. When he attacked again, he did so in a frenzy. He howled at the sky, then charged her, jumping and swiping, trying to land kicks, punches, and elbow strikes.

Cait blocked some with her hands, others with her legs,

and evaded a particularly wicked strike at her face with his claws. One of her blocks with the shillelagh got knocked aside, and by pure chance, the head of the stick smacked into her opponent's mouth. He recoiled, then spat blood onto the ground. Cait called, "First blood," but nothing changed. He continued to circle, and she kept her defenses up. "Hello? Anyone?"

The wolf across from her didn't seem to care that the condition to stop the match had been met. She pushed her emotions down and sought the cold center inside where her most vicious warrior lived. When he came in again, she used a quick block, followed by an elbow to his head to knock him back. She'd been unconsciously analyzing his moves throughout the fight, as Delsanra had taught her, and now had decent insight into what he might try. His next attack took her by surprise, knocking down that confidence, and she skittered to the side, keeping her weapon positioned between them. She said, "Stop now, or face the consequences of your actions."

He snarled and turned into his wolf form again, then leapt at her face, jaws gaping. She brought the shillelagh up, only to have it knocked out of her grip as he barreled into her, knocking her into a backward somersault. When she came up, she dove overtop him, back toward the middle of the circle, and was spinning and backpedaling as he launched himself at her once more.

Okay. Enough of this garbage. Cait gathered her magic and hurled it when he next jumped. That sent him flying upward, braying in fear. A moment later, her fireball intersected with his falling form. When he hit the ground, he was dead. She summoned her shillelagh, staring at the other members of his pack to see if anyone would try to take revenge for their fallen brother.

With a slow, condescending clap, the leader stepped forward. "Well-fought."

"So, the rules weren't really rules?"

He shrugged. "They were. He made the choice not to follow them."

Cait shook her head. "You can't have it both ways, puppy." His face twisted at the insult. "Be a part of the world, or don't. But don't think you can impose your apparently malleable definition of the rules on us."

He smiled and spread his hands at his sides. "Time will tell, witch. Thank you for providing the evening's entertainment. Now, get off our land."

She thought to say something pithy about how it wasn't really their land but decided against it. Instead, she replied, "You stay out of ours, or you'll face the consequences like your friend did." She walked calmly past him, toward the trees, in the direction of her village. She didn't need to look back since Aza kept up a running commentary in her mind, promising to warn her if they moved.

She hoped it would look like confidence to them.

To her, it felt like an unfinished job. *One that's going to require resolution sooner rather than later.*

CHAPTER TWENTY-FIVE

Yoshino Kyouka walked through the front door of the luxurious estate they'd borrowed for the meeting. Borrow wasn't quite the correct word. They had purchased the gambling debt of a wealthy businessman who'd gotten in over his head with one of the smaller gangs and now used his premises at will.

An advance team had made sure the place was secure, and she, her bodyguard Saito, and her second in command Kono climbed out of the limousine and walked up the long, shallow staircase toward the double entrance doors. Her kimono swished at her ankles as she held it up to keep it from the ground. The white makeup caking her face felt very old-world in this modern place.

She accepted a tablet from one of the servants a few steps inside that showed the displays from the cameras along the path her guest would take to reach her. Then she allowed herself to be led into the estate's most luxurious sitting room, where she leaned back in a comfortable chair with embroidered fabric and sipped from the cup of herbal tea set on the mahogany end table beside it. She asked Saito, "Is everything in readiness?"

He nodded. "All is as it should be, Madame."

"Is Kono irritated to be playing the role of escort?"

Her companion gave a low laugh. "I believe so, Madame. Likely more because I am in here and he is out there than the task."

She smiled at the information. "We must all experience discomfort sometimes lest we become overconfident."

In a question that would be bold for anyone other than him, he asked, "Even you?"

She laughed softly. "I would prefer to be in my garden, or perhaps a long bath, rather than meeting with a representative of an international assassins' organization. So, yes, even me."

Their conversation was stilled as another limousine pulled up in the view of the exterior camera. A figure stepped out of it, wearing a black business suit, white blouse, and shoes with thick heels. The woman glanced up at the camera as if she knew who was watching her. Yoshino followed the visitor's progress toward the sitting room and handed the tablet to her bodyguard in time for him to be in position by the door when their guest entered. Her second in command gestured at the chair opposite Yoshino, and the woman sat. He asked, "Would you like some tea?"

The newcomer gave him a thin smile and replied, in English with a noticeable Russian accent, "No, thank you." He stepped away, and the other woman turned her attention to her host.

Yoshino began, "Thank you for coming."

The woman shrugged. "I was in the States, so stopping by for a visit wasn't a serious imposition."

But you're implying it was a slight one. She smiled. "I'm happy to hear it. Are you sure you won't take some tea? It's ginger."

The visitor shook her head. Her shoulder-length blonde hair moved smoothly, catching Yoshino's attention for a moment. "I have only an hour. What would you like to discuss?"

She took one last sip of her tea and set it beside her. "A member of your organization. One Carl Winston."

The other woman's face didn't change. "I've never heard of that person."

Yoshino waved the comment away. "I assure you, on my word of honor, that this space holds no listening devices and I am not a representative of law enforcement." She smiled. "As I'm sure your research on me has shown. Please, let us speak frankly."

"That's not his name."

"Trivialities."

Her guest straightened as if preparing for a contest. "Very well. What would you like to know?"

"As you may or may not be aware, certain of his actions can be interpreted as placing blame on my organization for the killing he undertook. Judge Meyer's murder, to be precise. Who hired him?"

The blonde shook her head. "You must know I cannot divulge client information. I hope that's not the only reason you requested that I visit."

"Even though he was used to falsely implicate me?"

The other woman sighed and spread her hands. "For

any purpose. Discretion is one of the foundations of our business. And the intentions of our clients are not our concern."

Yoshino nodded. It was no more than she'd expected. "Are you aware he was imprisoned?"

"Yes."

"And killed in a riot?"

The woman's eyes locked on hers. "I have heard that said."

The words gave Yoshino hope. "Do I detect doubt about that outcome?"

Her guest smiled. "Our people are quite resourceful."

Yoshino took a sip of tea while she considered the information she'd received. "Hypothetically, if he was alive and I wished to hire him, would he be permitted to answer questions once contracted?"

The other woman gave a slight shake of her head. "Not about previous operations, which is what I imagine you're referencing."

That would've been too easy. "Would you say he is representative of your most skilled talent?"

Her guest laughed. "I would not. At best, he is second tier."

Yoshino nodded. "So, whoever hired him went cheap, relatively speaking. That sounds like the Roses." The other woman kept her face carefully neutral, but she thought she saw a slight upward twitch of her lips. "Let's leave him aside and talk about the future, then. If I wanted to hire one of your best, how would such a thing be arranged?"

They talked for a quarter-hour more. The woman departed as efficiently as she had arrived. Afterward,

Yoshino sat with a fresh cup of tea, and her two closest subordinates joined her, each with their own cup. After a time of silence to gather her thoughts, she said, "It was my guess that Rosetta wouldn't pay for the best. He never does."

Saito replied, "Clearly, what she provided is as much proof as we're likely to get of his involvement."

Kono nodded. "I agree. I think we can go forward with certainty that the Roses attempted to implicate us in the murder of the judge and reply accordingly."

Yoshino met his eyes. "What do you recommend?"

Her second in command shrugged. "An attack on one of their businesses that signals it came from us, and also that it's revenge for their attempt to malign our reputation."

"Give the task to someone you trust. Make it very public, but be sure only Rosetta knows it was us. We do not need the authorities suspecting our involvement."

"Yes."

Saito asked, "Are you considering hiring an assassin to go after Rosetta?"

She allowed herself a moment to contemplate the idea but shook her head. "Not at this moment, but it's always good to have resources. We must ensure an appropriate account is set up and funded should we need it."

Her bodyguard replied, "Consider it done."

"Very good." She finished her tea and rose from the chair. "It is time to get back to the city. There is a great deal to do now that Rosetta has reignited the war between our organizations."

CHAPTER TWENTY-SIX

Sabrina scowled at the phone on her desk when it buzzed with the sound of an external call. The display read "AET," which could be anyone from that office. She picked up the receiver. "Hello?"

"Hey, 'Rina."

She grinned. The person at the other end of the line was a professional friend she'd had lunch with now and again. "What's up, woman?"

"Got some information that's going to interest you."

"In a good way or a bad way?"

The caller chuckled. "That second, I'm afraid. One of the electronics you pulled out of the courthouse wasn't the same as the others, although it looked that way on the outside. Where most were only listening devices, further investigation revealed that this little baby is an infomancer relay."

Sabrina frowned at the phone. "This wouldn't just be a bad joke, would it?"

"No way. Why do you think it's me calling? Everyone else was too scared to tell you."

She laughed. "Please. No one's afraid of me."

Her friend replied, "That's because they don't know the true you as well as I do. But I figured you'd want to hear it right away. The report will land on your chief's desk later today."

"Thanks, sweetie."

"You know it." The other woman clicked off, and Sabrina pressed the buttons to shift her computer into auto-response mode. A bot she'd written would run in the background to answer questions that were simple enough for it to handle and put any others in a queue for her to address when she was done with the task that lay ahead.

She wandered to Chief Levitt's office and knocked on the door, receiving permission to enter. Sticking her head inside, she said, "Gonna do some magic. I'll be in the dungeon."

He nodded and looked over his computer glasses at her. "Anything I need to worry about?"

"Not yet. I'll let you know if it gets there."

Turning back to his computer, he said, "Good enough. Luck."

Sabrina closed the door and headed for her infomancy workspace. After locking the door behind her, she went into her dressing room and came out a few minutes later in her battle garb: a black t-shirt, big boots, and black leggings. She pulled her hair into a ponytail, wrapped a tie around it, and sat down at her computers, then tapped the keys to wake the system up.

Her brain was going a mile a minute. Half of it was

focused on how to deal with the issue, and the other half was incensed that it *was* an issue. Taking several moments to ensure that her hardware firewalls were active and functional and the software guards in the outer perimeter were too, she dove into the data streams.

The simulation that represented the marshals' computer systems in the Moakley, her personal territory, was a Gothic castle. It was a blend of styles she'd seen in films, from the *Nightmare before Christmas* through the *Addams Family* and on into *Dracula*. It had parapets, tall towers with spikes on the top, and an ominous black metal fence guarding it. The building was surrounded by a moat filled with crocodiles, the system's representations of low-level alarm bots.

She materialized in her office, which was adorned with paintings of war scenes on the walls interspersed with deadly-looking plants and flowers in dark pots on tall tables. She walked briskly from the room, searching for her chief sentry. Her high heels clicked on the stone floor, and she idly flicked the extra fabric hanging from the wrists of her vintage black dress as she traveled through the gloomy corridors.

Her castle had nine sentries, one for each point of the chaos symbol and the last for the center. The eight reported to the one, which served as the information funnel to her. All of them were sophisticated artificial intelligences, but the central one held the code she'd most intensively modified and improved. She walked into his chamber. He was seven feet tall, and he loomed over the space. His physical form had been inspired by the *Terminator* skeletons but was made of black iron. He held a huge sword, point on the floor, hands at his stomach on the crossbar of the pommel. When he saw her, he dipped his head in a formal bow. "Mistress."

She snapped, "Report on anything unusual you haven't already shared with me."

He paused as if thinking, doubtless reviewing his files. "The only aberration was an attack in the northeast, which held a signature we had not seen before. It did not penetrate the system or even subvert the outermost defenses, however, so the attempted intrusion was not elevated."

She replied, "Thank you," and walked the castle until she reached the northeast sentry. Without speaking, she rested a hand on his face. Data flowed in front of her eyes, and she scanned the logs until she spotted the occurrence. It was indeed a signature that had never tried to access the system before. Moreover, it was clearly a disguise. *So, an enemy infomancer took a shot at us. Bold. The reason it was different, in part, was because it came from the inside, evading my outermost defenses. Again, bold.*

She stepped back and traced a glyph, muttering words in Latin. A transparent palm-sized orb with a green crystal in the center appeared, and she gripped it in her right hand as she put her left back on the face of the guard. She closed her eyes and submerged herself in his recording, watching the attack on her systems. Her deft fingers spun the orb counterclockwise in her palm, and time reversed in the simulation.

She followed the infomancer's path until she found the source of the hack attempt. They had hidden their tracks well, routing through several proxy servers. However, they hadn't done as much as they should have since they hadn't expected the effort would be noticed. *And they would have been right if the hardware had evaded discovery.* She released her other programs and pushed herself into the simulation.

Space went white around her, then filled in section by section. When it was done, she was standing in the dirt between rows of grapes under a sunny sky, with rolling hills visible in all directions save one. There, a large house stood. Lifting her head and squinting into the sun, she summoned a broad hat and pulled its black veil down to cover her face and neck. She walked along the rows of grapes, one hand on either side, touching the fruit as she passed. It was a good simulation, though not on the same level of realism as her castle. *Perhaps it's not their home base, or maybe they've just got shoddy technique. If they work for the Dragons or the Roses, that wouldn't surprise me.*

When she reached the porch, an older man in a suit stepped through the screen door and gestured at the table, which had a pair of chairs on opposite sides. It supported a single yellow flower in a vase, an open bottle of wine, and two glasses on a white tablecloth. "Would you like a drink, Miss?"

Sabrina shook her head as she claimed one of the seats. "I'll wait for the owner, thank you."

The man nodded. "Of course. He'll be along shortly."

After only a few minutes, another man walked out of the house, tall and thin with a narrow, dark mustache, wearing a white linen suit over a blue button-up shirt. He greeted her, lifting her hand and kissing her fingers, revealing a French accent she thought was a little over-done. He took a seat and said, "So good of you to visit."

She replied, "Do you know who I am?"

He chuckled. "I have a guess." He picked up the bottle and poured red wine into his glass, then held it up and looked at it in the sunlight. "Would you like some?"

"Of course."

He filled her glass, and she sipped, her programs isolating and blocking the viruses contained within it. She smiled. "Nice try. Delicious, though. So, did you attempt to breach my castle on a whim, or were you ordered to do so?" She crossed her legs as she thought a wealthy person at a winery might do and adjusted the fall of her dark dress.

A frown flickered across his face. "I'm sure I don't know what you mean."

She smiled condescendingly. *This is a stupid game, so you're either stupid too, or pretending to be. Either way, you're annoying me.* "You think I came upon this place by random chance? Okay, but I've got the taste of you now." She raised the glass in a toast. "If I encounter it again, you can expect a much more substantive response."

He set his drink on the table and turned it slowly, both hands rotating the base as he peered into the wine. Finally, he looked up. "I see no reason to fear you."

She laughed and held out a hand, her programs summoning a simulation. A dark tan beetle with black spots materialized. "This is a grapevine beetle. Normally, they're no big deal. *My* pets, though, are a little more aggressive than the standard variety." She lifted her palm and blew on it, and the creature flapped its wings and headed for the grapes. As it moved away, it duplicated itself. By the time it reached the rows of fruit, a horde of identical insects accompanied it.

Sabrina stood and ran a hand down the front of her dress to smooth it. "Better hop to it. In an hour, they'll be chewing on your base code." She offered him a final smile. "Should we meet again, maybe you'll be wise enough to fear me."

CHAPTER TWENTY-SEVEN

Cait sat in the passenger seat of the sedan, thinking that Garrett was a *far* more sedate driver than Clement. True, they were not in a hurry, unlike her last few rides with the other man. Nonetheless, his piloting seemed more cautious. *Probably comes from having kids.* She complained, "This office has way too much territory to cover."

He laughed. "You're just upset because you can't zip-zap-portal everywhere all the time like you probably did in Columbus."

She frowned. "Get out of my head, Delsanra Copperfield."

"I think the Roses sent their ugliest person to meet that guard."

"Agreed." They had put their prisoner through the drudgery of looking through mugshots and surveillance photos of every known associate of the Roses and Dragons. By the end of it, he was only half-jokingly asking for enough morphine to put him out of his misery. He'd identified one, and after a good deal of digging, they were driving through the countryside to visit him.

She remarked, "Sabrina is really good at what she does, sorting through all those different addresses to see which ones were active. She's way better than the guy we had in the Columbus office."

He nodded. "No argument. She's fantastic."

Something in his voice caused her to look at him accusingly. "You don't think he'll be out here."

He laughed. "Nah. This is probably his mom's house or something. This is totally going to be a broken lead. But at least it's sunny out, so a nice day for a drive."

She scowled. "Damn. Wish we could've called ahead."

"And warned him?"

She crossed her arms and indulged in a pout. "I didn't say it was a good idea."

He laughed. "This is the job, sometimes." Her phone vibrated as she received a message and continued to vibrate. She dug it out of her inner pocket and saw a string of numbers that sent energy shooting through her. She sat up, all humor gone. "Stop the car. SOG summons. I must go right now."

He pressed the brakes and pulled over to the side of the road. "This happen often?"

She popped her seatbelt, opened the door, and climbed out quickly. "More often than you think." She slammed the door, conjured a portal to her landing place at Camp Beauregard, and stepped through. She exited the closet and held up her phone, tapping the button to connect with Elliot Black. He came on immediately. "Spirit, are you here?"

"Affirmative."

"Good. Everyone's on the way to their pickup points. Get them here as fast as you can."

She walked toward the locker room. "Got it." They practiced this process every three months, and Cait thought the ability to bring everyone together quickly was the perfect argument for including a magical on each team. If not that, at a central location. Sadly, the marshals weren't that progressive about magicals, not even the SOG. Her phone buzzed, and she activated it. "Yeah?"

An upbeat male voice that sounded young emerged from the speaker. "I'm Kendall, and I'll be your infomancer today."

She laughed at the patter, which she'd heard more than once from the magical computer experts the marshals accessed to assist in their ops. Usually, they came from the NSA, but in the past, they'd also had people from the National Guard, the Army, and even Homeland Security. She replied, "Who's first?"

Two had been at the base, Elliot "Knight" Black and Tori "Brain" Lawson. That left nine for her to transport. The locker room felt claustrophobic when everyone had gathered, less because of the number of people in it than due to the energy they carried. Elliot ordered, "Gear up. Full urban kit. We'll brief on the way." He and his second in command left the room while the rest of them got to it since they had already dressed.

She banged open her locker and pulled off the skirt,

blouse, and jacket she'd been wearing for her day job. Beside her, Angel remarked, "Hey, nice necklace, Spirit."

She laughed. "This old thing?"

Kingston "Royal" Foster warned, "Devil, you keep looking at Spirit like that, and your wife's gonna take a knife to your *cojones.*"

He made an obscene gesture at the team's medic, earning a laugh. They'd all long since lost any sort of modesty around one another and were as close as brothers and sisters. Sure, sometimes emotions ran hot and could be mistaken for attraction, but nothing would ever come of it. Especially between her and Angel, who almost always wound up teamed together.

She pulled on her urban fatigues, which were a white and gray digital camouflage pattern, over a black t-shirt. She fastened it to her neck and at her left wrist but left the right one unbuttoned, rolling up the cuff once so her bracelet was free.

Next, she slipped on her equipment belt, which held an abundance of standard gear, including a pair of metal tubes containing a healing potion and an energy potion. She bent to step into her boots and lace them up, then tucked the bottom of the fatigues into them since that part of getting ready was far easier to do before she donned the rest of her gear.

She tied down the holster to her right thigh, then strapped the plate carrier around her body. It was custom-fitted to her, comprised of combination ceramic and metal plates in the front, over the ribs, and on her back. They had been formed to her shape, and the oversized vest fit snugly.

It *was* bulky and slightly hindered her in hand-to-hand combat, but not enough to matter.

She patted her belt to ensure the combat baton that substituted for her shillelagh was present, then grabbed her helmet and slammed the locker door. She walked into the adjoining room, where the unit's armorer stood in the opened weapons cage. He recognized her on sight and handed over her STI 2011 pistol and M4A1 rifle. She said, "Gas grenades and beanbag gun, please."

The man nodded and stepped away. Aza took that moment to ask, *Is this normal?*

She replied, "Pretty much. Could be something, could turn out to be nothing. We always deploy as if it'll be the most dangerous thing we've ever faced. It's in a place where civilians might be around, which is why we're in urban gear, so I'm adding nonlethal grenades and the shotgun to my standard stuff." She accepted those weapons from the armorer; the canisters were in a bandolier that went over her shoulder and crossed her chest, and the truncated shotgun clipped to her equipment belt at her left hip.

She looped her rifle over her chest, shoved the pistol into its holster, and went to find Elliot. He was waiting in the hall outside. "Good, you're ready. We're going to need your taxi service again. One second." He stuck his head in the locker room and yelled, "Two minutes, people." Returning his attention to her, he said, "Get us to the Baltimore airport."

She nodded. "On it, boss." Once he'd discovered how valuable her ability to portal was, he'd sent her on a tour of the airports on the east side of the country so she could learn them and be able to transport the team there. She concentrated on recalling the feel of that location. *This is where a portal beacon would come in handy. I need to think about how that might work.*

She waved her arm and whispered the word to open the portal, and through it, she saw that the sign she'd requested had been posted where it should be, confirming that she'd connected to the right spot. She called, "Good to go."

CHAPTER TWENTY-EIGHT

They left the portal location at a fast jog, arranged in two side-by-side lines, and headed for a pair of waiting helicopters. She wondered if they'd fly to DC, or if their target was in Baltimore or somewhere else. Team B split off, leaving Cait with the core she trained with most often: Knight, Brain, Devil, Royal, and Crystal. *The teams need to work together more frequently. One more thing to suggest for summer training.*

They piled into the aircraft, and when everyone was on board, they lifted off. Over the helmets' comms, Elliot said, "Okay, people, listen up. An FBI informant put in an alert about the gang he's part of. The group's leader, who's been absent for some time, is suddenly back in town, bragging about an op they're planning to pull off tonight. One that's going to involve 'A lot of bodies.'"

Cait growled and saw similar feelings expressed on the faces of her companions. "The group is headquartered in a storage building. We're working on finding out all we can about it, but for now, assume we might find anything inside. Our primary goal is to break up the action. Whatever they're planning, we can't let it happen. Secondary goal, almost as important, is to take out the leader. He's on the fugitive list and clearly needs to be removed from regular society. Finally, if we can, we save the informant. They'll identify themselves by using the word 'Phoenix.' Any questions so far?"

Brain, the team's second in command, asked, "Do we know how long they've been holed up in there?"

Elliot shook his head, then relayed, "Uncertain. We've got several infomancers on the job, but this was put on in a hurry, so they're playing catch-up. They cracked the nearby cameras and are doing what they can to identify traffic flows in and out of the building. However, with enough people, or the right disguises, or a magical to transport by portal? This could be anything from a false alarm to a nightmare."

Angel spoke up. "If it's the second one, I'm just the Devil to bring it down around their ears." The team laughed at his bravado, and even Elliot managed a smile before resuming the briefing.

"Team B will disembark first and switch to vehicle transport for ground-level attack. We're going in from the roof. It's an eight-story building. The inner layout shows an outer corridor on the perimeter of each level, as well as a central inner lane. Team B will surround the target to cover the exits and apprehend anyone who tries to flee. We've got a solid chance to get them all, according to the informant, because the leader has called everyone in."

Brain commented, "Bad choice on their part."

Elliot nodded. "But good for us, and for all the people they plan to kill tonight." The somber note inspired silence in them all. After a moment, he finished, "All right, any last-minute thoughts?" No one had any. The team exchanged confident nods, reinforcing their solidarity, then they verified the readiness of weapons that had been checked any number of times.

A female voice joined the channel. "I'm Tabitha, and I'll be your infomancer for this operation. Standby for integration."

Every member of the team wore large aviator-style glasses that served a triple purpose. First, they were made of a bulletproof material that would hopefully keep their eyes safe from attack. It wasn't perfect, but it was far less distracting than wearing goggles. Second, they could operate in low light and thermal modes when paired with the comm unit each carried on their belts.

Their third, and arguably most important, function, was to serve as a HUD, a heads-up display. A map appeared on the far left of her visual field, a vertical rectangle showing their position in relation to the destination, along with a clock counting down their estimated arrival time. The system pinged her weapons, which returned status information that showed on the far-right side of her vision. M4A1, thirty rounds. 2011, twenty rounds. Four grenades. Six beanbags in the revolver-style drum.

She'd never seen what anyone else's displays showed, but the team's medic, Kingston "Royal" Foster, had said his provided medical data on the team, gathered from sensors on their plate carriers and the glasses. She imagined that

Julie "Crystal" Schorr had customized information on engineering and communication, her specialties, as well.

Elliot said, "All right. Cable up and get ready."

Each member of the team grabbed a strap that was secured to a carabiner on the floor on one end, with the remainder coiled up and attached to the walls or ceiling. She removed the coil closest to her and threaded it through the appropriate loop on her belt, then flexed her hands in her tight leather gloves in anticipation of the need to grip it to control her descent.

The pilot came over their comms. Her voice was crisp and commanding. "Not going to land, not going to stick around. We pull up, you slide, we're gone. If you're not detached, you get to come along for the ride."

Elliot replied, "Understood."

"Fifteen seconds." The doors had been open throughout the flight, and buildings were visible below. Cait patted her weapons to be sure they were secure, then stepped onto the landing bar. She gripped the handhold mounted on the craft's side for that purpose with one hand and locked the other on the descent line. Angel climbed out opposite her, and Julie took the position between them.

The chopper stopped and rocked, killing its momentum like a bird flapping its wings, and she jumped. The line whipped through her fingers, and she quickly descended the fifteen feet to the rooftop and ripped the rest of the cable through her belt, setting it free. A motor pulled it back up as the helicopter flew away. She looked around, noting with satisfaction that all six of them had made it safely.

Elliot reported, "Team A in position."

Dominik Lane, the other team's commander, replied, "Team B, one minute out."

Crystal stated, "Scanning."

The infomancer's voice cautioned, "I don't trust that stairwell."

Crystal replied, "Me neither. Recommend an alternate entry plan, Knight."

Elliot offered, "Okay, we'll go down the sides. Three teams, standard deployment." Cait crossed the distance to Crystal and accepted a small explosive charge, a rectangular box with an adhesive side. Tori did the same for her team. Devil rigged a line around an HVAC unit on the roof and slid three carabiners onto it.

Each member of the team attached their personal line, which was coiled inside their belt, to one of them. A schematic of the facility appeared in her glasses, and she noted where the windows were. Elliot ordered, "We'll go in from the north side. Brain and I will take the left hallway, Crystal and Royal, the right. Devil and Spirit, that puts you in the center."

Cait chuckled. "Boss, everyone knows the left-hand side is the evil side."

He quipped, "Yeah, but you balance him, so that leaves you in the middle."

"Fair enough."

The infomancer said, "I'm not getting any useful scans from inside the building. Can you amplify your equipment?"

Crystal replied, "Negative. It's on max. Hopefully, we'll send more when we get inside."

They moved into position at the edge of the roof, then

at Elliot's "Go," they lowered themselves over it to walk down the side. She placed the explosive when she and Angel were positioned on opposite sides of their window. "Ready."

Two more readies echoed theirs. Team B reported in place, and Knight said, "Team A, *go go go*."

CHAPTER TWENTY-NINE

The explosives detonated simultaneously at a signal from Julie, and Cait pushed off and swung inside. She hit the button to cut the line and landed in a crouch facing the central hallway, the rifle in her hands tracking the half-circle forward and to her right. Angel was beside her, doing the same on the other side. She reported, "Spirit and Devil in position."

Tori echoed her, followed by Kingston. The infomancer said, "Stand by." A moment later, she continued, "Still nothing. I'm reading the floor plan well, but the storage units are holes of nothingness."

Angel replied, "Meaning, they're empty?"

Julie clarified, "Or shielded really effectively."

Elliott ordered, "Deploy mobile sensors." Cait dipped a hand into her belt and came out with a small orb. Angel did the same. They rolled the devices down the central hallway. The floor plan in their glasses increased in resolution as the sensors confirmed existing information and added more. The video feed, which was stabilized algorithmically, showed that each storage area was fronted by a large blue garage door and had a numeric keypad mounted on the side.

Cait asked, "Do we have a master key?"

The infomancer growled, "We do not. The company wants a subpoena."

Angel snarled, "Don't get me started on lawyers."

Cait had juiced her senses before jumping down, but she couldn't penetrate the storage areas either. She whispered, "Aza, anything?"

He answered, *I hear movement below, but nothing nearby.*

Julie said, "I've got no readouts, nothing. Collect the marbles and head downstairs?"

Elliott responded, "I'm not comfortable leaving these at our backs. We need to open them."

Kingston replied, "You're the boss, boss."

Cait moved to the door on her right and set one of the marshals' electronic code breakers next to the keypad. It took fifteen seconds before the keypad flashed and the garage door slid upward to reveal an empty bay. She muttered, "Well, that's anticlimactic."

Angel laughed, and they moved on to the next pair of doors after the one on his side also revealed nothing. After they'd opened two each, and the other teams had done the same without incident, Cait said, "I've got a bad feeling about this." Normally she expressed information gathered magically as a feeling, so the others tended to listen when she used those words. This time, it was just a worry.

She muttered to herself, "Stop being an idiot, Cait," and moved to the side, where an attack from inside the unit wouldn't hit her. She motioned for Angel to do the same, then summoned a wall of force in front of the next garage door. The lock breaker pinged, the door rolled up, and again, nothing happened. She looked around the corner quickly and saw another empty bay.

She switched off her mic so only Angel could hear her and said, "I might be paranoid." He shook his head, a serious expression on his face, and gestured at the next. When the door went up, a claymore detonated, shooting ball bearings out to slam into her force shield and clatter to the floor. She thanked her subconscious for keeping her honest. They reported in, and the others stopped what they were doing and retreated to where they'd entered.

Elliott asked, "Still no useful readings?"

Julie and the infomancer replied in unison, "Negative."

He nodded. "Okay, here's what we're going to do. I hate leaving this level without clearing it completely, but there's no point in exposing ourselves to additional traps if we don't have to. We'll guard the stairs while Crystal and Royal go up and spike the door to the roof so no one can use it. Then we'll descend, exit on the seventh floor, and spike that one, too."

Brain cautioned, "Cutting off our retreat."

"I know, but we can afford the extra few seconds to blow the doors if we have to. Better that than getting attacked from behind."

His second in command replied, "Works for me."

Elliott warned, "Keep an eye out for traps in the stairwell."

As they were making their way down to the next floor, the infomancer reported, "I'm finally in the building's network. It's been hacked. The security cameras aren't showing you. All the records from the last month are the same, according to my software. No people visible."

Dominik Lane's voice broke into their headsets, sounding agitated. "We've got action on the ground floor. They're shooting from the windows. Civilians have been pushed back, and the police perimeter is moving out a half block. We've got solid defensible positions, but if they have heavy weapons, a breakout is possible."

Elliot snapped, "Tabitha, status on backup?"

She replied, "AET in seven minutes. SWAT is twenty out."

Dominik responded, "Understood. If they make a break for it, we'll let you know."

Elliott answered, "Acknowledged. Team A, we need to move faster."

They emerged from the stairwell at one corner of the building and immediately found themselves in danger. Cait, on point, shouted the alarm, dropped her rifle, and swept her hand in a semi-circle, snapping out the commands to invoke her force shields. The turrets mounted from the ceiling at the corners of the building fired salvos down the long hallways that intersected at the stairwell.

The impacts of the rounds on her defenses sent shudders through her body, but her shields held. She growled, "Back up and get out of the line of fire." Her team complied, and she retreated out of the turrets' firing arcs. The one on the left stopped shooting, but the one ahead, apparently inspired by the open door, continued its barrage. The rounds were coming fast, but fortunately not at machine-gun speed.

She pushed her shield forward to intercept the bullets before they reached the intersecting hallway, then focused her will to keep it in place. She leaned out of the doorway and fired a sustained burst of lightning down the left corridor, prepared to pull her arm and head out of the way if the turret reactivated. Her electrical attack struck something vital, and when the weapon tried to fire, it whined and smoked but no bullets emerged. She advanced into that hallway and angled the shield so she could cast past it, then did the same to the other turret. She said, "Let me do some recon before you come out."

Angel replied with a snort, "Yeah, you do that. That's a great idea."

She moved ahead and discovered the center aisle wasn't covered by a turret. *Unexpected bonus.* "Anything from the sensors?"

The infomancer answered, "Nothing. Big empty boxes. I'm fairly certain it's because they're shielded, not because they're empty."

Kingston replied, "Well, you're just full of good news, aren't you?"

She looked into the far corridor and saw a pair of turrets in the corner at the opposite end, one pointing down each hallway. She ducked the initial hail of bullets, then shielded and destroyed them both. "Okay, we're ready to move forward."

They took their positions again, with her and Angel in the middle, and rolled the orbs they'd retrieved from the floor above down the corridors. The sensors added detail to the displays, though, as before, little of it was useful. Cait said, "Okay, moving down the center." The first unit held another claymore, which detonated into her force shield.

Echoes of explosions came from the other hallways, as well, but each team reported being okay. As they worked on the next door, Aza warned, "I hear something." She threw up walls of force on all sides of them, locking them in a cube just in time. Ahead of them, five doors banged open simultaneously, and enemies flooded into the hall. Four dashed out of sight at the far end, two pairs heading in different directions.

The remaining quartet lifted weapons. Two held wands, the other two guns. The bullets bounced off her shields, as did the lightning and flame attacks, then the pair wielding pistols let the magazines drop out of them. She growled, "Magicals. Watch out. Aza, go protect the others. Devil, let's go kick their asses before they get their anti-magic bullets loaded."

CHAPTER THIRTY

At Cait's command, Aza left her neck. Each flap of his wings increased his size as he headed toward his target. He wanted to stay and attack the people who were threatening his companion but understood that her experience and knowledge outweighed his. *For now, at least.*

At the end of the hall, he turned left, then accelerated, knowing he was racing the bad guys. He took the next corner at speed, pouring every bit of strength he had into making his wings beat faster. He arrived to see two members of Cait's team, one of them the joke-filled doctor, hurling grenades at enemies. His partner shouted, "Into the storage unit," and they backpedaled and rushed through an open garage door.

That choice suited Aza. When the wizard at the far end sent the gas away before it could do any damage, he raced forward and breathed fire on the pair. The wizard summoned a shield to block his attack from reaching them, then water poured from the ceiling, shooting out of small nozzles.

Aza spun and flew away from the pair to make another pass. He felt an impact, then a burning, biting sensation all over his body. His wings failed to work and he crashed to the floor, then slid down the slick tile surface until he reached the far wall and slammed into it. His sudden descent made the wizard's sustained attack lose its target, and he huddled for a moment with his wings drawn up protectively around his head, waiting for the pain to stop.

When it happened, the pain vanished all at once. More than that, his scales shimmered, becoming silver and metallic. He'd never heard of such a thing and had not experienced it before, but he instinctively knew that he'd just gained some measure of defense against the attack he'd undergone. He chuckled. *Something tells me you're about to wish you hadn't done that.*

He threw himself to his feet, and when the wizard tried the same attack again, Aza spread his wings in front of him as a shield. The lightning refracted from his scales, shooting off in all directions. He walked steadily down the hall until the wizard abandoned the lightning, then launched into the air again.

His allies hadn't been idle in the interim. After a brief pause while—as he imagined it—they adapted to the reality that a dragon was in the building with them and decided he was an ally, they had started firing rifles down the hall-way, interspersed with more grenades. Aza saw the shimmer of the wizard's shield where it met the mist from the grenades—and that it failed to fill the space. The edge near the wall didn't quite reach. The shield was oriented on the wizard rather than the area he was trying to guard. *Oops. Bad move.*

Aza shrunk to pass through the gap, then landed and grew larger as he bit the leg of the nearest enemy. It wasn't the wizard, unfortunately, but when Aza whipped his head around and hurled the man into the back wall, he struck with a satisfying crunch. The wizard looked at him in shock, and Aza gave him a toothy grin. It was the last thing his enemy saw before flame ended him.

———

Cait focused on maintaining shields to protect her and Angel from the wizard's attacks as she dashed forward. There was no time to switch to anti-magic bullets, and she made a mental note to ensure that one of her SOG weapons was loaded with them in the future. She let the rifle fall and drew her baton with her left hand, flicking it in a quick circle to extend it.

Trusting Angel to handle the mundane opponents, she eliminated them from her strategy, although she kept her senses sharp in case her partner should fail to remove them quickly. She reached the first wizard, who seemed surprised that the battle had come to him. She whipped her baton in from the left in a forehand strike, but he projected a beam of force from his wand, turning it into a long stick with a spike on the end, and blocked her blow with it.

Cait growled, "Oh, you're fancy," and spun toward the other magical. When she finished the spin, she put the strength of her enhanced muscles to good use as she jumped and delivered a front kick at the wizard's face. He managed to get an arm in the way, and the limb snapped under the impact of her boot. He tumbled backward with a cry, and she growled, "Hope that was your wand arm, jerk."

She couldn't take the time to finish him because of the other one. A bullet whizzed past her head and she flinched, but it was her partner taking down one of the other gunmen. She turned the flinch into a quick shuffle to her right so the wizard had to turn to keep her in view, then whipped her baton up between his legs. He blocked with his force stick, then shoved the pointed end toward her face.

Cait stepped to the side, marveling at how easy it was to evade his untrained efforts and snapped a low kick at his knee. He brought the weapon down reflexively to block, which gave her an opening. She filled it with a punch, her fist landing solidly into his temple. He staggered sideways and banged the other side of his head on one of the storage units' garage doors, then collapsed.

She searched for the other wizard and saw that he was standing nearby, cradling his broken arm and crying in pain. She spun into a back kick, and her heel landed on the back of his skull and pitched him forward. The blow dazed him, and he made no effort to catch himself as his face smashed into the floor. She laughed, hearing her mother's voice in her mind saying, "I'll give you something to cry about."

After taking out the wizard, Aza threw himself around the corner and headed for the far end of the building. His speed took him past the center hallway in a flash, allowing him only a single glimpse to confirm that Cait was still fighting before he was past. He'd known that since his sense of his partner told him *how* she was as well as where she was.

He could read her emotions from a distance. They came strongly enough that he imagined he could detect them from farther away than he could speak to her. She could only speak to him with her outer voice, which was a problem he would urge her to solve soon since it hampered their ability to be effective partners.

He rounded the corner and took in the scene. The two non-magicals had gone down to Knight's bullets or those of his partner. His allies were leaning around the outside edge of a storage locker, shooting at the wizards. The magicals had their wands raised, at least one of them focusing on defense, as evidenced by the force shield protecting them. The hallway was scarred with the scorch marks of fire and lightning, and the other wizard was levitating a fireball in preparation for sending it down the corridor.

Aza considered blasting them with his fire, but he thought it might be worth having one to talk to, so he barreled into the wizards and canceled their spells. His allies popped out of the hiding place and eliminated the wizards with a flurry of shots. *Maybe we don't need to talk to them.* He flew past, rolling once in the air, then rejoined Cait. Her fight was over, and he landed beside her. She said, "Aza, this is Angel, as you know. Angel, this is Aza."

The man Aza found to be funnier than the rest replied, "So, you have a necklace that turns into a dragon. That's totally normal."

Cait laughed. "Technically, it's a dragon who turns into a necklace."

The man said, "Oh, that makes it much better. Lucy, you got some 'splainin' to do."

The words, said in a thick Spanish accent, caused Cait to laugh again, and Aza made a mental note to find out why. The rest of the team appeared in the hall, and Cait introduced them. Knight said mildly, "If I'd known we had a dragon among our assets, I might've planned differently."

Cait replied, "Are you saying I'm not enough?"

The funny one who was also a doctor said, "You know, this place sucks. Maybe we shouldn't hang around chatting."

The leader nodded. "Okay, people. Next level."

CHAPTER THIRTY-ONE

The next floor was a copy of the one above it, and turrets engaged them as soon as they arrived. Cait took care of the first without exiting the stairwell by calling up a shield to protect her, then blasting lightning through a small hole in its top.

Julie said, "Wait one," which stopped her from going after the next. "I think I've got their wireless signal." A couple of moments later, she continued, "Oh yeah." The sounds of turrets firing came from elsewhere on the floor, and she laughed. "No one to shoot in the outer aisles, unfortunately. Lacking other targets, I had the turrets shoot each other. It was *deeply* rewarding."

Cait chuckled, and they moved forward and split into the same groups as on the other levels. Aza stayed out of sight behind her, ready to assist anyone who called for help. Before they could advance, heavy security gates crashed down from the ceiling to seal off the outer halls, leaving them only the middle corridor, which they had not yet reached, as an option. The infomancer reported, "Lots of heat signals in the hallway. At least a dozen. Plus, several units aren't reading anything, like the ones above."

Elliott said, "Let's take a look," and rolled his sensor orb past Cait into the center corridor. The feed popped up in her glasses, showing a space filled with objects pulled out of storage to create hasty bulwarks and firing positions. She saw several enemies before a burst of gunfire killed the feed.

She asked, "Frontal assault?"

Elliott replied, "They've prepared the battlefield, which doesn't bode well for us. Can you get the two nearest storage units open without jeopardizing yourself?"

"Sure." She reached out with her magic and ripped the closest blue door upward. It revealed no enemies, only an assortment of junk stacked inside. She cast a shield to block the hallway's opening and dove across it, somersaulting before throwing herself the rest of the way to safety. Gunfire slammed into the wall as she released the shield behind her, but none of it caught her. She repeated the process on the other door, yanking it upward to reveal more stuff. *How is it people have enough things that they need to get storage lockers and I'm living in a hotel? Doesn't seem fair.*

A laughing voice called from down the hall, "Very impressive. You defeated the ever-so-dangerous garage doors. Well done. Now, call it a day and go away."

She exchanged glances with Angel across the opening. Elliott replied, "We thought we'd invite you to come with us."

"No thanks, we're good. You all just toddle along."

Elliott's voice hardened. "You can't get out of here.

Whatever you had planned is over. Time to surrender before you all wind up dead."

The unseen man laughed again, sounding unreservedly happy. "That's fine. Killing some marshals will be worth it."

The infomancer spoke into Cait's ear. "New wireless network just activated."

Julie snapped, "What is it? I'm seeing it, too."

The infomancer replied, "Not sure yet."

Cait asked, "How does he know we're marshals?"

Elliott shook his head. "No idea. Cameras, maybe. Or, since he's a fugitive, he knows we'd be the ones to respond."

Aza warned, "Sounds from the left and right hallways."

Cait offered, "They might be trying to flank us."

Elliott ordered, "Brain, with me. We're left. Royal, Crystal, you're right."

Kingston quipped, "As usual," then deployed as ordered.

Angel gestured at the hall between them. "Guess that means it's us for the center."

"Guess so. You want to lead?"

"You're the one with the big magic shield. You go first."

She grinned. "Coward."

Her partner laughed. "I prefer to think of it as being smart. Perhaps you're not intelligent enough to understand." She cast a force shield in front of them, and they moved down the hall in a fast shuffle, taking advantage of the cover provided by the enemy's barricades to avoid their firing lines. When one popped up to try his luck, Angel shot at him and she threw lightning, and their target went down.

She warned, "Gas," and threw a grenade. *Wish I'd*

brought a launcher instead of the shotgun. Lesson for next time. The grenade went off, then came flying back down the hallway at them as an enemy magical repelled the attack. She waved it into one of the storage areas she'd opened, where it would be out of the way. They'd pulled their gas masks up on the previous level, so it was no threat to them. Belatedly, she called, "Aza, be careful of the gas."

He laughed in her mind. *Figured that out, thanks. Smells terrible.*

When they reached a point where they could get no closer while staying behind cover, Angel asked, "You ready, Spirit?"

"You know it, Devil. I'll lead this dance. Aza, be careful, and do what you can."

His tone was serious as he replied, *Count on me.*

Cait charged around the barricades she'd been crouching behind. The first line of defense was mundane; she grabbed her enemy's rifle barrel as it swiveled toward her, stopping it before it became a threat. Her left fist flashed out, connected with his face, and dropped him.

Angel, a step after her, was already past and engaging the next one in line. He rammed his rifle forward and up, holding the stock in one hand and the barrel in the other, to smash the enemy in the throat with it. That man fell, and Angel dipped to one knee and fired at the next target who'd been foolish enough to remain uncovered.

Cait grabbed another canister and hurled it down the hallway, then did the same with her last one. Aza flew overhead, and gunfire chattered. He barked, "Ouch," and curved around to land behind her.

Fear spiked. "Are you okay?"

He replied, "Only a graze. I'm not bulletproof, it seems." His voice brightened a little. "I might be immune to lightning. You see, during the last fight —

"Not the time, buddy."

The leader of Team B reported, "Security grates just came down around the building. It's sealed off from the outside on the bottom level."

Elliott replied, "What the hell are they up to?"

The infomancer sounded alarmed. "More signals just lit up. They're coming from the whole building, connecting to the new network." Foreboding ran through Cait as he said, "Holy hell, it's wired to explode."

She snapped, "Meet in the back of the central corridor," and called a shield to seal off the hallway, then ran back, trusting that Angel would be behind her. At the end of the corridor, she turned toward Elliott's position to get out of view of the enemy and opened a portal, instinctively choosing the location she'd used last—the airport in Baltimore. She shouted, "Go go go," and the others ran through it.

Before she or Aza could follow, the explosives went off.

The blast wave sent her flying. Later, she would say that Fate was looking out for her because instead of slamming into a wall, she hurtled through a window. It hurt a lot because the windows were heavy security models, but the force of the explosion slammed her through the multiple panes.

The impact stole her consciousness, so she only knew what happened next because someone outside had a cell phone aimed at the building. She flew out and fell, and a moment later, Aza barreled out of the window, growing larger as he moved, and sank his talons into her leg to slow her flight. He couldn't lift her, but he set her down on the ground gently rather than having her splatter against it after a six-story fall.

Consciousness returned in a haze of pain, and she realized she was burned from the explosion. She fumbled at her belt, wondering why she couldn't see well. A concerned voice she recognized from Team B asked, "What do you need?"

She choked out, "Vial. Potion. Red." The pain in her face was agonizing now that it had made its way into her awareness, and she could only imagine how bad the burns must be. When her teammate poured the liquid into her mouth, a wave of cool healing flowed through her. A few moments later, after drinking the whole flask, she was able to sit up with assistance. Part of the building had collapsed, and the rest was on fire. "They really didn't like us if they went to that much trouble to try to kill us."

Aza, who was flying but could apparently still hear her, replied, *Seems like there's a lot of that going around lately.*

She laughed, wincing as her healing skin pulled painfully. "True that, buddy."

CHAPTER THIRTY-TWO

The healing potion worked, but Elliott insisted she visit the hospital. Cait had enjoyed an ambulance ride, with Aza back around her neck, then several hours in the emergency room getting checked out. When she was finally released, she portaled back to the base to drop off her gear, then went to the hotel for a couple of hours of sleep.

Friday morning was spent in a debrief with the SOG, during which she stayed silent except to answer questions directed specifically at her. That broke up at lunchtime, then it was off to the marshals' office for a Friday afternoon meeting to wrap up an eventful week.

After everyone was seated, Chief Levitt tossed a newspaper on the conference table. On the front page, a brightly colored picture showed Cait dangling from Aza's talons. She'd avoided all media since the incident, fearing something like this might happen, and she groaned. With a barely suppressed smile, Simon asked, "Got anything you'd like to tell us, Cait?"

The others laughed. She replied, "You knew about the dragon."

Garrett said, "Yeah, but we didn't know he could do *that*. Like, why aren't we riding *him* rather than driving around in cars like primitives?"

Aza's laughter, which had started the moment the newspaper landed, continued unabated as the other marshals offered outrageous ideas about how the dragon could help them do their jobs.

Finally, Sabrina asked, "Are you famous now? Can I have your autograph?"

Simon took the reins of the meeting back. "Okay, seriously, what did you learn this morning?"

She replied, "The fugitive, Michael Strail, was captured by the marshals before. It's likely he carried a grudge. They're still investigating whether it was a trap for the SOG or if a real action was planned."

Clement frowned. "Confirmed kill?"

"They're going through the rubble, but the likelihood of knowing for sure is small. Even if they find bodies, chances are good that he burned in the fire."

Simon frowned. "Better watch your back. The whole SOG team, in fact."

She nodded. "I hear you. Any word on Winston?"

He shrugged. "Case closed, as far as the prison investigation goes. Died in the fire."

"Do you believe that?"

Garrett replied, "Could be we *all* need to watch our backs for that dude. Or his ghost if he's dead since we put him there." The meeting broke up in laughter again, but it was darker this time.

On the way out, Sabrina stepped to her side and said in a low voice, "Maybe portal in and out of your new place. I'll hide the records of you being there. You know, just in case."

Cait nodded. She'd been thinking along similar lines. "Good plan." She spent the evening moving stuff from one place to the other, then portaled to her village. She got there in time for breakfast and chatted with her dad about his research on the Drow while the others arranged the food and beverages.

Once everyone had assembled, the conversation turned to the shifters. Brianna said, "Things in Westport are even tenser."

Her mother nodded. "Word is that the shifters have visited individual families at home and demanded they leave. Same with the shops, and they've been seen in the public spaces, too."

Aisling folded her arms. "Well, that's got to stop."

Cait sighed. "They won't be happy until the whole island belongs to them."

Lewis added, "They're not going to quit pushing until they get it."

Moira shook her head. "Then it's up to us to stop them. Fate works in mysterious ways. To face a threat like this, the coven voted the right family into leadership."

Leonard Rosetta climbed out of the back of a large sedan with tinted windows and nodded at his bodyguard, who closed the door behind him. They walked up the sidewalk toward a modest suburban home, one of many identical models in a massive housing development. His organization owned several and used them as hideouts since they were far enough outside the city that most wouldn't think of looking for them there.

When they entered, the occupant lowered the pistol that had been pointed at the door and shoved it into the back of his pants. Rosetta asked, "Now, is that any way to greet your rescuer?" He followed the other man into the kitchen.

Carl Winston pulled open the refrigerator, withdrew three bottles of sparkling water, and set two of them on the counter. He uncapped the last and drank before replying, "You got me out, as we agreed you would if things went bad since you're the reason I hung around. Our contract is done. Once I've healed, our relationship is over." His face was covered in blisters, and he walked with a slight limp.

They had indeed gotten him out, but not before he'd taken some damage from the fire, which had proved more robust than expected. *I need a better demolitions expert.* "I've got another contract for you."

The assassin shook his head. "I'll be taking some time off."

Rosetta nodded. "Sure. I understand. Take a week, then get back to work. I want you to kill Yoshino Kyouka."

The other man lifted an eyebrow. "She's very well protected. If I was dumb enough to take the gig, it would cost you plenty."

"I'll pay you what I was paying before, but this time straight to you. No syndicate."

Winston thought for a moment before replying, "It's not unprecedented, but that might make them angry."

Rosetta waved a hand like he was pushing the worry away. "I'll risk their displeasure. So, will you do it?"

Winston shrugged. "Maybe. We'll see."

Rosetta smiled. "I anticipated that might be your response, so let me sweeten the offer. Once you kill Yoshino, I'll deliver the marshal that put you in jail into your hands."

A slow smile crept across the assassin's face. "Then we have a deal."

Cait Keane and her Dragon partner Aza are surrounded by powerful enemies. The peace between the Roses and the Dragons is over and the streets of Boston have become a dangerous place as the hidden war escalates. Continue the adventures in *WITCH WITH AN ENEMY*.

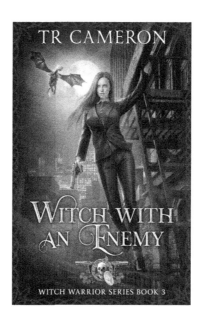

Claim your copy today!

AUTHOR NOTES - TR CAMERON

MAY 13, 2022

Thank you for joining me for book two!

Important note: I've written a Cait short story for you to enjoy, about her earliest days with the Special Operations Group. You can find it here: https://BookHip.com/DPKPMTF. It's yours for the minor commitment of signing up for my newsletter. I have absolutely no problem if you want to then unsubscribe for my newsletter. But with social media as quirky as it's been of late, I'd love to have a channel to communicate with you that I can depend upon.

The amount of lead time involved in the writing process is a weird thing. I finished this book, the second in the series, a week or so ago, and the first one won't be out for another 12 days, I believe (Or around there. Anyone who attends our First-Friday lunches on zoom knows exactly how on top of release dates I am. Hint: not so much).

The four beta readers who gave me feedback on the first volume helped me make some important changes.

They seemed to enjoy the characters and story, though, so it gives me hope that our readers will, as well!

My conference travel was surreal. After not being in an airport for two and a half years, it all felt very strange. Being one of a few people at the conference who was still masking was also odd. I might be over concerned, or I might just be very aware of my own mortality and questionable health. Either way, no one hassled me, I hassled no one, and a great time was had by all. Plus, I brought back some valuable insight to apply to my day job.

Speaking of travel, I'm set to attend the 20books conference in Vegas in November, including the author signing / sales day. So, if you're local, be sure to stop by and say hi!

I crashed and burned into the end of the semester and academic year. Just too much going on, and me more or less unable to keep all the balls, knives, and flaming torches I was juggling airborne. I'm starting to climb out of the wreckage now, but it's slow going.

One of the things I managed to get done was to pick up some hand-me down couches from family to replace our 10-year-old-falling-apart Ikea couch. We loved that one and would have gotten another but a) it's not available anymore, and b) the recommended replacement is also unavailable because of supply chain, weather, divine intervention, or some other unknown reason. The reason I mention it is that right now, while I sit on couch one typing, there are four cats lying on the other one sleeping. They clearly approve.

I decided during the writing of book two that we'd have to visit Aza's family again. I'm looking forward to writing that reunion. He's a strange mix of goofy and confident, which I put down to age and the fundamental (deserved) arrogance of dragons. Since starting this series, I've taken to spending a lot of my time in Fortnite burning down buildings. There could be a connection.

My need for reading escapism has sent me to John Scalzi yet again. I'm rereading the *Old Man's War* series, and it reminds me why I like his writing so much. It's ultimately grounded so well in the characters, who are usually sassy, snarky, and just somehow real. Even the aliens. It makes me think that I need to allow my own characters more time just to chat about things. Several of the books are also written in first-person, which kind of appeals to me. I'm too wary of changing voice to do it in my urban fantasy though. But if I ever get that Nylotte fantasy series off the ground, maybe that's the place to try it out.

I saw *Dr. Strange and the Multiverse of Madness* in an actual theatre. It was lovely to be back in one. The movie was good, and heart rending. I'm not sure if I'll be able to watch it again; the depiction of trauma was harsh. I also saw *Sonic 2* in the theatre. Jim Carrey is a treasure when he's doing the kind of characters that really only he can do. Watched *Coraline* on the small screen, and it's kind of shocking it took me so long to get to it. It was wonderful.

Still slogging through *Moon Knight*. I'm just so bored. The plot is intriguing, but they spend so much time on one feature of the character that I just can't. But I will finish it. Eventually. I did manage to finish *Book of Boba Fett*. After four episodes it's almost like they said, "You know, this isn't going so great. Let's do something else." The something else worked.

I've started watching Our Flag Means Death and it's clear that I just don't get what's popular these days. I don't feel the buzz. Next episode the amazingly brilliant Taika Waititi joins the cast for real, so maybe that will change my opinion. But it's about as slow as *Boba Fett,* which is extra bad for a comedy, I think.

So it's time for me to get it in gear on book 3. Got the first amusement park trip of the summer on deck next week with the kid, and they're going to be sucking up a lot of my time before and during, because there's planning, and packing, and all the other fun stuff you do proximate to a road trip. I'm excited to get to adventure again. Wishing you all good things until our paths come together once again.

Standard monthly reminder - If you're not part of the Oriceran Fans Facebook group, **join**! There's a pizza give-away every month, and Martha and (usually) I and all sort of fun author folks show up via Zoom to chat with our readers. It's a great time, and the community feel to it is truly fantastic. The group is very welcoming and enthusiastic. Oriceran Fans. Facebook. Your phone is probably within reach. Do it!

Before I go, once again, if this series is your first taste of my Urban Fantasy, look for "Magic Ops." I promise you'll enjoy it, and you'll get more of Diana, Rath, and company. You might also enjoy my science fiction work. All my writing is filled with action, snark, and villains who think they're heroes. Drop by www.trcameron.com and take a look!

Until next time, Joys upon joys to you and yours – so may it be.

PS: If you'd like to chat with me, here's the place. I check in daily or more: https://www.facebook.com/ AuthorTRCameron. Often I put up interesting and/or silly content there, as well. For more info on my books, and to join my reader's group, please visit www.trcameron.com.

This post is about working through the roller coaster ride of post-chemo. Not an easy trick, but doable.

Chemo has changed a lot in recent years and for the better. The newer versions you get to keep your hair and it doesn't almost kill you. It's more like having a mild flu with a lot of weird symptoms.

Most people around me don't really know something is off. I work at looking my version of normal. (My version of normal behavior is always questionable. Might be why Michael is fond of saying I based the troll on myself. Fair assessment.)

The truth is I'm generally in mild pain, maybe some nausea and the muscles in my hand may be twitching – along with a laundry list of weird side effects. It is what it is and it's not uncommon – but like I said – doable.

It's been about seven months since I stopped taking chemo, but the drugs stay in your body doing their job for another two years or so. I prefer to say one year and hope for the best but there it is. These days I like to say I'm going through chemo withdrawal. The shocked look on people's faces as they resort through the words is worth it.

This all means that for at least another year the side effects rage on, up and down and for some time to come. One week I feel a glimpse of some kind of normal. Maybe not what I was pre-chemo but better and my heart feels lighter.

But the next week they may come roaring back and with a new twist. The kind of chemo I was on turns your immune system on high and leaves it there. The drugs are tailored to identify cancer and kill it but at the same time it's a stew of chemicals that cause inflammation. Lots of systems go haywire – in big and little ways. Mild vertigo, flushed cheeks, nausea, fatigue, shortness of breath, muscle spasms, buzzing in my ears. You get the idea.

I funnel it all into a book with new ways to torture the villains. It makes me feel better when they get hit with a fireball and go up in cinders.

The reality is some days it's harder to put words on paper and takes longer to do and can feel defeating just for that reason. And yet I keep going and words still add up to a book.

At 62 years old (despite Shayne Silvers saying last week he thought I was in my forties – the man can write some good fiction), I've learned something about all kinds of adversity. It comes and it goes and in between I keep on living. Otherwise, too much time would be spent on the sidelines.

I walk slower, take more naps and type slower, but I still go – because my efforts at the end of the day and week and month, add up to something. It's a remarkable lesson to learn. My efforts and who I am are actually enough.

It's also made me really appreciate the friends who have stepped in and helped, often without me even asking for anything. It's another lesson I've learned. Help is very appreciated and creates tighter bonds for both sides. I love more than I can the cards and letters I've gotten from fans, and people like Charley Case who showed up magically by my side on loan from his wife, Kelly and cooked and fixed things for a week. It made everything easier even after he was back home in Idaho because I knew I wasn't really ever alone.

One last lesson so far is when I'm doing what I love like writing, or gardening, or playing with the dogs, I forget for just a little while how I feel. It doesn't all fall away but it's not front and center – and things get done. It's remarkable that even in the midst of struggle it's still possible to have a good life. More adventures to follow.

OTHER SERIES IN THE ORICERAN UNIVERSE:

THE LEIRA CHRONICLES
CASE FILES OF AN URBAN WITCH
THE EVERMORES CHRONICLES
SOUL STONE MAGE
THE KACY CHRONICLES
MIDWEST MAGIC CHRONICLES
THE FAIRHAVEN CHRONICLES
I FEAR NO EVIL
THE DANIEL CODEX SERIES
SCHOOL OF NECESSARY MAGIC
SCHOOL OF NECESSARY MAGIC: RAINE CAMPBELL
ALISON BROWNSTONE
FEDERAL AGENTS OF MAGIC
SCIONS OF MAGIC
THE UNBELIEVABLE MR. BROWNSTONE
DWARF BOUNTY HUNTER
ACADEMY OF NECESSARY MAGIC
MAGIC CITY CHRONICLES
ROGUE AGENTS OF MAGIC

OTHER BOOKS BY JUDITH BERENS

OTHER BOOKS BY MARTHA CARR

JOIN THE ORICERAN UNIVERSE FAN GROUP ON FACEBOOK!

CONNECT WITH THE AUTHORS

TR Cameron Social

Website: www.trcameron.com

Facebook: https://www.
facebook.com/AuthorTRCameron

Martha Carr Social

Website: http://www.marthacarr.com

Facebook: https://www.facebook.com/
groups/MarthaCarrFans/

Michael Anderle Social

Website: http://lmbpn.com

Email List: http://lmbpn.com/email/

https://www.facebook.com/LMBPNPublishing

https://twitter.com/MichaelAnderle

https://www.instagram.com/lmbpn_publishing/

https://www.bookbub.com/authors/michael-anderle